From the way his sister looked, Luke knew he was in trouble

"What's wrong with you?" Rachel asked without pre-amble.

"Wrong?"

"Yes, genius. Kealey's been assigned as caseworker to the kids. Which means she has control over whether you can keep them." Her tone grew caustic. "Couldn't you have dipped her hands in acid, or set fire to her shoes to *really* show your feelings?"

Exasperated, Luke stared at his sister. "She was on the date with me. She *knows* we didn't hit it off."

"If there was the slightest possibility she'd forgotten, it was certainly diplomatic of you to remind Kealey that you can't stand her."

"Do you think she'll hold it against me?"

"You'd better hope not. For the children's sake."

Luke glanced toward the living room. In a matter of hours he'd turned his life upside down. And now the fate of three innocent children depended on whether he could change his tone with Kealey Fitzpatrick.

He shook his head, knowing he had a better chance of getting rid of h͟i͟s͟ ͟s͟i͟s͟t͟e͟r͟ ͟b͟e͟f͟o͟r͟e͟ ͟s͟h͟e͟ ͟d͟r͟o͟v͟e͟ him crazy.

Dear Reader,

As a hopeless romantic, I am always drawn to a hero who protects and inspires. Luke Duncan is that kind of hero. Protector of children and animals, he is a man without equal.

Enter stage left, a heroine who no longer believes people with integrity like his exist. Throw in three orphans, a menagerie of pets and strays, and you have *Substitute Father*.

This book is special to me for many reasons. I hope you will fall in love with the characters as I have, perhaps even reserve a spot in your heart for the pets who love us for who we are, rather than who we wish to be. And, most of all, I hope you enjoy the journey I'm about to take you on.

Sincerely,

Bonnie K. Winn

Books by Bonnie K. Winn

HARLEQUIN SUPERROMANCE
898—THE WRONG BROTHER
964—FAMILY FOUND

Don't miss any of our special offers. Write to us at the following address for information on our newest releases.

Harlequin Reader Service
U.S.: 3010 Walden Ave., P.O. Box 1325, Buffalo, NY 14269
Canadian: P.O. Box 609, Fort Erie, Ont. L2A 5X3

Substitute Father
Bonnie K. Winn

TORONTO • NEW YORK • LONDON
AMSTERDAM • PARIS • SYDNEY • HAMBURG
STOCKHOLM • ATHENS • TOKYO • MILAN • MADRID
PRAGUE • WARSAW • BUDAPEST • AUCKLAND

ISBN 0-373-71019-4

SUBSTITUTE FATHER

Copyright © 2001 by Bonnie K. Winn.

All rights reserved. Except for use in any review, the reproduction or utilization of this work in whole or in part in any form by any electronic, mechanical or other means, now known or hereafter invented, including xerography, photocopying and recording, or in any information storage or retrieval system, is forbidden without the written permission of the publisher, Harlequin Enterprises Limited, 225 Duncan Mill Road, Don Mills, Ontario, Canada M3B 3K9.

All characters in this book have no existence outside the imagination of the author and have no relation whatsoever to anyone bearing the same name or names. They are not even distantly inspired by any individual known or unknown to the author, and all incidents are pure invention.

This edition published by arrangement with Harlequin Books S.A.

® and TM are trademarks of the publisher. Trademarks indicated with ® are registered in the United States Patent and Trademark Office, the Canadian Trade Marks Office and in other countries.

Visit us at www.eHarlequin.com

Printed in U.S.A.

Dedicated to my brother, Gary Yedlovsky,
a true hero in every possible way.

CHAPTER ONE

Greenville, Texas

LUKE DUNCAN IDLY scanned the metallic streamers that hung over the cash register of the grocery store's film counter. It looked to him as though the booth contained enough lottery tickets for half the smallish town.

"Feeling lucky?" the clerk asked, following his gaze to the lottery tickets.

Luke glanced at the sacks of groceries resting in his cart. "Actually, I need to pick up my pictures. Name's Duncan."

She nodded and turned to a drawer holding the developed film. As she did, he maneuvered his cart to the end of the counter to clear a path for the other customers. It was clever of the store's management to position the film and lottery counter so close to the exit. The location made it easy for patrons who had already paid for their groceries, to pause and purchase a bit of the state-run fantasy.

"Did you say Duncan?" the clerk asked, sifting through the drawer.

He leaned over the counter, trying to read the names on the plump yellow envelopes. "Yes, Luke Duncan. I brought in my film about a week ago. I had two rolls."

"Here's one of them," the clerk announced, placing the packet on the counter.

Eager to look at the photos, Luke opened the envelope, letting the pictures spill out into his hands.

The clerk rummaged a bit more, then spun back around with the other packet in her hand. Her flirtatious smile faded as her brows drew together. "Isn't that your cart?"

Distracted by the pictures he was viewing, Luke didn't glance up. "My cart?"

"Look!" She pointed toward the exit.

Belatedly, he saw what she was talking about. "What the…?"

Luke spotted a young boy wheeling his grocery-filled cart out the door. Shock held him still for a moment, then he hollered. "Wait!"

The boy turned for an instant. But instead of slowing down, he began to run, pushing the loaded cart across the lot with remarkable speed.

Luke watched for a few seconds in disbelief, then fumbled with the slippery pictures filling his hands. Dropping the photos on the counter, he barely paused. "Keep an eye on these, will you?"

The clerk, looking equally dumbfounded, nodded.

Luke tore off toward the door, still unable to believe the boy was stealing his groceries. That sort of thing didn't happen in their midsize Texas town. Greenville was big enough that you didn't know everyone, but small enough that you could leave a cart of groceries unattended and expect it to be safe. But that same cart of groceries was barreling across the busy street.

Luke sprinted the length of the parking lot, but the light was red when he reached the curb. Fast-moving cars and trucks filled the road since it was shift change at the local machine works factory.

Luke's feet scarcely remained on the concrete as he waited to cross the street, determined to catch the little thief. But when the light changed and the traffic cleared, the boy wasn't in sight.

Cursing to himself, Luke thought he'd lost his quarry, but then he caught a glimpse of the cart as it whipped around a corner. Luke bolted across the street, gaining speed as he neared the spot he'd last seen the cart. But when he turned into the alley, it was empty.

Then his eyes narrowed. One screen door in the deserted lane stirred ever so slightly, possibly the result of being slammed shut. Luke approached cautiously. It occurred to him that the boy might not be working alone. Perhaps it was a ruse orchestrated by an adult who wanted bigger pickings than groceries.

His gaze alert, Luke pushed open the door. It was dark inside, but as his eyes adjusted to the dim interior, he could see that it appeared to be an abandoned store. Empty metal racks and cardboard boxes were scattered through the musty space. But there were no signs of an ambush.

Still, Luke didn't lower his guard as he stepped farther inside. Then he spotted it—the shiny metal of a grocery cart gleaming through the dust motes. Although it was partially pushed behind a curtain, there was no mistaking the distinctive buggy. The kid was clever, but not clever enough. He'd picked the wrong sucker to steal from.

Luke ripped open the curtain. "All right you..." The words died away as Luke stared at the young robber. The terrified boy stared at him defiantly as he shielded two younger children, a boy and a girl. As Luke fumbled for words, the girl burst into tears.

The child who had stolen his cart pulled her closer, but she continued crying.

Luke knelt down, patting her shoulder. "It's okay now, no need for tears. No one's going to hurt you." Then he met the oldest boy's eyes. "Why don't you tell me what this is all about?"

For a few moments the boy stood mute, his mouth set in a stubborn line.

Luke, however, didn't back down.

Finally the boy wavered a fraction. "You didn't need this stuff."

Seeing how frightened the children were, Luke kept his tone mild. "That's not the issue. I want to know why you stole my groceries."

"They gotta eat!" the boy burst out.

Luke stared at the child, a sickening pit forming in his stomach. "What do you mean?"

"We don't have no food," the youngest boy explained.

The pit in Luke's stomach hardened. "Were you planning to take the groceries home to your parents?"

The oldest boy momentarily looked panicked, then his mouth thinned again, a determined if futile gesture.

The younger boy wasn't as stoic. "We don't have no parents."

For a moment, Luke just looked at the children. "Why don't you tell me your names?" he urged finally, heartsick at their plight.

"I'm Troy," the youngest boy offered.

Luke nodded, then smoothed one hand over the girl's matted hair. "And how about you?"

"Hannah," she managed to say, her tears beginning to subside.

Luke leveled his gaze on the oldest boy.

Reluctantly the child spoke. "Brian Baker."

"And I'm Luke Duncan. Where have you been staying?"

Brian's gaze traveled to a few ragged sacks on the floor.

Luke had to take a deep breath to hide his shock. Luckily the August nights were warm, otherwise the kids could have become seriously ill. Straightening up, he withdrew his cell phone. "I'll call the police and get you some help."

"You can't do that, mister!" Brian hollered, before Luke could dial.

"You can't!" Hannah echoed, then started sobbing again.

"Whoa!" Luke replied. "I just want to get you some help."

"They'll separate us!" Brian shouted. "We can do just fine on our own!"

Luke's gaze encompassed the bare, dirty space. "I can see that. But if your parents abandoned you—"

"They didn't!" Brian shouted in reply.

"Mama *died!*" Troy told him. "She wouldn't just go off and leave us!"

Even more perturbed, Luke slowly lowered the phone. "When did she die?"

"Couple weeks ago," Brian answered sullenly. "They were coming to take us away when we left."

"Maybe the authorities had found relatives who could take you in. That doesn't mean you'd be separated."

"They were going to put us in foster homes," Brian replied. "*Separate* foster homes. We heard 'em."

"What about your father?" Luke asked gently.

"He died a long time ago," Troy told him solemnly. "When I was borned."

Luke glanced from face to face, seeing pain, terror

and worse—a disheartening lack of hope. No doubt they were hungry and tired as well. "Okay, I won't call the police. For *now*."

Brian looked suspicious but relieved.

Luke considered his options and knew he had only one. "You're all going home with me."

"We don't want nothin' from you," Brian asserted. "We'll pay you back for the food."

"I have a better idea. We'll take the groceries to my house and cook some supper. Then you can help me figure out how to work my PlayStation."

Although Troy looked intrigued, Brian was still resistant. "We're fine here."

Hannah hiccuped. "I'm hungry."

Obviously torn, Brian stared first at his younger sister, then at Luke.

Taking charge of the situation, Luke tugged the cart from behind the curtain, turning it toward the door. After shifting the groceries, he picked up Troy and deposited him in the cart. Then he lifted Hannah to rest on his hip. Luke kept his tone mild as he met Brian's gaze. "You coming with us?"

With no other choice, Brian nodded.

"Where are your things?" Luke asked.

Brian shrugged and again Luke felt his heart constrict. Not even a change of clothes among them. "Traveling light has its advantages."

Brian nodded, but Luke could see the boy's throat working, either from gratitude or shame. Casually, Luke draped one arm over Brian's shoulders. "I'll need your help to get the younger ones across the street.''

Brian straightened up and nodded, obviously relieved to be assigned some responsibility. Briefly, Luke wondered at the hand of fate that had placed these kids in such a predicament. Then he concentrated on getting them out of the alley.

It didn't take long to get them into his Bronco. Luke wasn't certain if it was fatigue or fear that kept the children quiet once inside.

Within a few minutes, Luke drove the short distance from the grocery store, then stopped the SUV in front of his rambling, old Victorian home. The large house looked imposing, but he'd purchased it for a song, doing most of the renovation and restoration work himself. It had proven perfect for both his home and his veterinary practice, which was located in the front of the house.

"You live *here?*" Troy asked, obviously impressed by the proportions of the house.

Luke unbuckled their seat belts. "Yep. It gets kind of drafty in the winter, but otherwise it's okay.''

"Okay..." Brian repeated in awe, staring up at the third-floor dormer windows of the attic.

Luke wanted to chuckle at their reaction, but realized the children would think he was laughing at them. Instead, he handed each one a sack of groceries, then shepherded them up the walk.

Once inside, they stared upward at the impres-

sively tall ceilings. Luke remembered a similar feeling when he'd first stepped inside the house. Then
it was run-down, in danger of being condemned. But
he had seen past the ramshackle condition to the
possibilities contained beneath layers of peeling
paint, torn wallpaper and threadbare carpet.

"Put the sacks on this table," Luke instructed,
showing them an old drop-leaf hall table that had
once belonged to his grandparents.

Although they complied, each one was trying to
take in the unusual house.

"Who else lives here?" Brian asked, still gaping.

Just then several dogs started barking ferociously.
All three children turned to stare.

"That you, Luke?" Wayne Johnson called out
from the clinic portion of the house.

"Yep! Come on out here."

Curtained French doors swung open. A fortyish
man stepped out, wiping his hands on a towel. The
volume of the dogs' barking increased with the
opening of the doors. Wayne carefully looked over
the trio of children. But he didn't show more than
mild surprise. "Howdy."

The kids responded with a variety of greetings.

"I don't suppose you all are here to help me with
the critters," Wayne commented.

Luke smiled, realizing his assistant had accurately
assessed the situation. His calm demeanor was helping defuse the tense atmosphere.

"Critters?" Troy asked.

"Yep. Dogs, cats, a raccoon, couple of ducks and even a snake."

The kids faces reflected varying shades of fascination.

"Snakes are icky," Hannah announced. But the boys didn't look as though they agreed.

Relieved to hear her speak without crying, Luke sent his assistant a look of gratitude. "Tell you what, guys. If we can talk Wayne into giving you the grand tour, I'll start some supper."

"Be my pleasure," Wayne told them. "Course I might need a volunteer or two to help with the ornery animals."

Their eyes grew even rounder as they trailed Wayne into the clinic.

Not bothering with the groceries, Luke strode quickly into the kitchen. In moments he was dialing the phone. His sister, Rachel, a social worker for the county, answered her office phone on the first ring.

Quickly he filled her in on the situation.

"Do you want me to send someone to pick them up?" she asked, concern filling her voice.

He paused. "Actually, Rach, I want to keep them here until you can find their relatives. That shouldn't take too long. I was hoping you could get me some sort of temporary permission."

"Why you?"

"They've been through so much already. They're scared to death of being separated. They were tired, hungry. And if you could see their faces…"

Rachel's own compassion was felt in the sigh that reverberated over the phone line. "Enough said. I'll see what I can do."

"Thanks, Rach. Oh, do I need to call the police, let them know the kids are here?"

"No, I'll take care of that. If they're telling the truth, there'll be a record of the mother's death."

"Why would kids lie about a thing like that?"

"You forget, I've seen more kids in trouble than you have."

"Granted. But I don't think these kids had any trouble until their mother passed away."

"Maybe not." She hesitated. "Luke, you've been bringing home strays, animals *and* people, since preschool. Don't get too attached. This won't be more than a temporary solution."

"Yeah, I know. And that's all I want. You're bound to turn up some relatives soon. But until then, someone needs to give them a break. Besides, I have a sister in Social Services who can pull a few strings."

"Actually, I think that's called a conflict of interest. I can probably get you the temporary permission, but I can also guarantee that if anything more is involved, my supervisor will assign the case to someone else faster than the ink can dry."

"Do what you can, sis."

"Don't I always?" Rachel questioned wryly. "I'll get back to you as soon as I can."

After thanking her, Luke retrieved the groceries

from the front hall and started cooking. Having been raised with seven brothers and sisters, he'd learned early on how to cook huge meals. While he chopped and diced, Luke called his oldest sister, Mary. Hearing about the orphans' plight, she offered to bring pajamas and clothes, which was what he had been hoping she'd do. Since she had five children of her own, she had plenty of hand-me-downs.

Soon the aromas coaxed the children back from the clinic to the kitchen. Luke's dogs, Bentley, a golden retriever, Miles, a border collie mix, and Ginger, an undefinable mix, followed them. His cats, Spencer and Kate, made separate appearances.

It was clear from the children's ravenous appetites that they'd missed many meals. They'd barely finished eating when his sister Mary and her oldest daughter rang the bell. Apparently, Mary had called his other sister, Ruth, who came by shortly afterward with three of her children.

There was something about a big family that defied quiet.

In typical Duncan fashion, the house vibrated with noise as they opened boxes filled with clothes, blankets, pillows and toys. Not much later, his brother, Peter, arrived in his pickup truck. It was loaded with a set of bunkbeds his children had outgrown along with a twin bed he'd collected from another brother, Matt, who had ridden along to help unload and set up the beds.

The children looked overwhelmed by all the people and attention. Just then the doorbell rang again. It was Rachel, his younger and favorite sister.

She shook her head as they entered the living room, gazing at the confusion. "How'd they find out about the kids?"

"My big mouth," he admitted. "I was just hoping for pajamas and a change of clothes."

Rachel didn't restrain her chuckle. "You *know* what they're like. Didn't you tell them this was just for a few days?"

"Yep. I don't think anyone was listening, though." His gaze sharpened. "I hope you're not here in person because you have bad news."

She screwed her face in a noncommittal expression.

"Rachel?"

"It's not exactly bad."

The doorbell rang yet again.

Luke swore briefly beneath his breath. "What now? Or should I say *who* now?"

"Luke—" Rachel began.

"In a minute. I'll get rid of whoever that is and be right back."

Luke yanked open the door, but his greeting was never uttered.

Kealey Fitzpatrick stood on his front porch, looking as stiff and uncomfortable as she had on their disastrous blind date months earlier. But what was she doing here?

Then it struck him. He turned to stare at Rachel, who had trailed him to the door.

"I tried to explain," Rachel began.

"Explain?" he growled.

"I told you the case would probably be assigned to someone else."

Someone else, yes. Kealey Fitzpatrick, no. The woman had the warmth and personality of tumbled marble. Still, he kept his voice low as he turned back to Rachel, so that only his sister could hear. "If this is some sort of convoluted way of trying to fix me up with her again—"

"No, Luke. It was just the luck of the draw. I didn't have any control over who my supervisor chose."

He groaned, then turned back to Kealey, reluctantly opening the door wider. "Come in."

She hesitated, but only for a moment. "I will need to speak to the children." Glancing past Luke, Kealey met Rachel's eyes in silent acknowledgment.

"They're in the living room." Luke closed the door, then led her inside. He hoped she wouldn't snatch them away tonight, eager to put them in some cold institution.

Kealey paused as they stepped across the threshold. It seemed noise and movement came from every square inch of the room. Mary and Ruth didn't skip a beat, continuing to outfit the kids with clothes and accessories. It was something Luke was accustomed to.

But Kealey seemed to pale at all the chaos. She turned to Luke. "Which ones are they?"

Since Brian, Hannah and Troy were surrounded by his nieces and nephews, Luke could understand Kealey's confusion. "I'll introduce you."

He did, and the noise subsided considerably.

Before the children could grow fearful of another stranger, Kealey smiled gently at them. "Hi, I'm Kealey."

Three small heads bobbed up and down cautiously.

Her smile, warm and reassuring, surfaced and Luke stared at her in amazement. He hadn't guessed she possessed any warmth. As quickly, it occurred to him that she might have a difficult time keeping her job if it became known that she was cold and uncaring with kids.

Kealey knelt down beside the children. "Can you tell me how you're feeling?"

"Okay," Brian answered for the trio, still assessing her.

"We're going to help Luke with giving them baths," Mary offered with a tentative smile. "And we've brought over pajamas."

"Fine," Kealey replied, before turning back to the children. "Then maybe we can talk some more."

Luke leaned close to Kealey. "Could I speak to you for a moment?" Not waiting for a reply, he cupped her elbow, guiding her out of the room and into the entry hall. "Look. They've had a helluva day. Can't we wait till tomorrow for the third degree?"

Something flickered in her eyes and he wondered if his words had penetrated her icy exterior. Surely they hadn't offended her, had they?

Then she spoke and he dismissed the notion. "Fine. I'll be back in the morning."

He walked her to the door, drawing it open. "I'm sure you will."

Again that unfathomable expression flickered deep in her eyes and then was gone. She nodded, turning away.

Closing the door, Luke turned around. To his surprise, Rachel stood in the hallway. And everything about her stance promised trouble.

"What's wrong with you?" she asked without preamble.

"Wrong?"

"Yes, genius. Kealey's been assigned as caseworker to the kids. Which means she has control over whether you can keep them on a temporary basis, or if she'll insist on putting them in a state home." Her tone grew caustic. "Couldn't you have dipped her hands in acid, or set fire to her shoes to *really* show your feelings?"

Exasperated, Luke stared at his sister. "She was on the date with me. She *knows* we didn't hit it off."

"Well, by all means, if there was the *slightest* possibility that she'd forgotten, it was certainly diplomatic of you to remind her that you can't stand her.''

"Rachel, that's a bit extreme. What I can't figure out is why you ever set me up with a cold fish like her. More importantly, why you'd want her for a friend.''

"That's the point, isn't it?'' she retorted. "You didn't bother to find out.''

"Granted. But Kealey didn't want me to get to know her. She was equally relieved to have the date end.''

"That's not exactly a glowing review of you, either!'' Rachel reminded him.

"So it's not.'' Luke hesitated. "Do you think she'll hold it against me?''

"You'd better hope not. For the children's sake.''

Luke glanced back toward the living room. In a matter of hours he'd turned his life upside down. And now the fate of three innocent children depended on whether he could change his tone with Kealey Fitzpatrick.

He shook his head, knowing he had a better chance of getting rid of his older sisters before they drove him crazy. And from the increasing noise level in the other room, that, too, would be damn near impossible.

CHAPTER TWO

KEALEY FITZPATRICK hitched up the strap of her shoulder bag. After rechecking her skirt, she made certain her jacket was straight, then smoothed her hair. It was ridiculous to be nervous, she knew. After all, this was just another case, another group of children who would probably be inducted into the foster care system. Then why had she been unable to sleep the previous night, caught up in thoughts of Luke Duncan?

In fact, when their supervisor had assigned her to the case, Kealey had immediately questioned Rachel. Although Rachel denied having anything to do with their supervisor's decision, Kealey was skeptical. Rachel had always been disappointed that her matchmaking efforts between her brother and Kealey had failed. Somehow she had thought that complete opposites should attract.

But that only happened in the movies. Despite her nerves, Kealey smiled. That was her solitary, secret vice—beautiful, romantic movies, especially those from the black-and-white era. Funny. Color, much like real life, intruded into the fantasy.

Climbing the steps on Luke Duncan's porch,

Kealey adjusted her purse strap yet again and rang the bell. After considerable time had passed, she pushed the button again.

However, when the door was suddenly yanked open with more force than she expected, Kealey nearly toppled backward.

Luke Duncan stared for a moment. Then to her surprise, he rearranged his expression into a more pleasant one. "Morning, Kealey. Won't you come in?"

Nodding, she stepped inside.

Since he still looked distracted, she managed a small smile. "Is everything all right?"

He shrugged. "Just a little debate about clothes."

Kealey glanced at his casual jeans and T-shirt in question.

Luke's expression grew a bit exasperated. Then his face cleared as he managed a faint chuckle. Stepping aside, he revealed Troy who was clad in a striped purple-and-green shirt paired with red-and-yellow plaid pants.

But Kealey didn't respond as he expected. Instead, her face brightened as she walked up to the youngster. "Looking good, Troy."

He grinned. "Thanks!"

She smiled as well. "Do you remember me from last night?"

He nodded. "Uh-huh. Are you Luke's girl-friend?"

Taken aback, she cleared her throat. "I'm with

the county Department of Social Services. We make sure children are well cared for.''

Troy shrugged skinny shoulders. ''Luke's taking care of us okay. We don't need nobody else.''

Her gaze flew to meet Luke's.

But he didn't qualify Troy's comment. ''How about some coffee?''

''This is a professional call, not social.''

''Don't professionals drink coffee?'' Luke asked with ease, his lips curling upward.

Kealey felt herself tighten and wished she had the ability to relax, to take life as easily as most other people did. ''Well yes, but—''

''Come on into the kitchen.'' Luke took her elbow, eliminating her need for a response. ''Coffee's fresh and strong.''

''Did you have trouble getting the children to bed?'' she asked, accepting the mug he offered, dragging her gaze from the appeal of his dark, sleep-tossed hair and handsome features.

''Nope. They were so tired they could have slept on rocks. Not that they had to,'' he hastened to explain. ''As you saw last night, my family brought over some beds.''

Kealey thought of Rachel's fuzzy family stories, how she'd deliberately ignored them. ''That was generous of them.''

''I asked for pajamas and got the complete setup for three. Beds, clothes, toys, you name it, they brought it over. Of course, along with the help comes the advice." He pinned her with an even stare. "And I'm not really in the market for advice."

Kealey stiffened. "Despite what you may think, I take my job very seriously—"

"I never doubted it."

"And as such, I'm responsible for the children's welfare. That means their care and how it's administered."

Luke met her eyes and for a moment she thought he would protest. Instead, he shrugged. "Then you'd better check out what they're eating for breakfast."

Momentarily distracted, she glanced around the tidy, if masculine kitchen. While the house didn't resemble the sleek contemporary interiors of many bachelor pads, it was clear its resident was all male. No fussy curtains draped the large bay window or the long, tall glass panes over the aged copper sink.

Also evident were the clean lines of the mission table that dominated the center of the farm-style kitchen. It, too, was unsoftened by fabric covering. Nonetheless, the room was incredibly inviting. Perhaps it was all the bright sunshine or the spacious dimensions. She glanced away from Luke's searching gaze. She supposed it might have something to do with the house's owner.

Hearing the other two children approaching, she glanced toward the doorway. Brian held his younger sister's hand. Even though it was apparent he took a protective role in regard to his younger siblings, she could see the fear disguised beneath a cultivated layer of bravado. And she was an expert at recognizing that particular fear.

"Hello," she greeted them. "Do you remember me from last night?"

Brian nodded warily. "Yeah."

"I'm here to see how you're doing."

Both children stared at her suspiciously. Then Luke turned away from the stove, his attention focused on her as well.

"I'm with the Department of Social Services," she explained.

Dead silence greeted her words. The only betraying action was the flexing of Brian's hand as he clutched Hannah's more firmly.

Luke filled the gap. "We're having scrambled eggs, guys. Everybody take a seat and we'll start with some milk."

Although Brian entered the room, his distrustful gaze remained on Kealey. Casually she glanced at the half glass Dutch door at the rear of the kitchen, wondering if the boy was calculating an escape plan. Also wondering how she was going to connect with this one.

"Brian, you take charge of the toast," Luke told him. "Bread and butter's on the counter. I've made six pieces, we'll need four more. Hannah, see if you can find some jelly in the fridge."

Reluctantly the children parted to obey him. Troy was distributing plates and silverware rather unevenly on the table. As he did, Luke handed him one more plate, then placed a platter of bacon in the center of the table, not commenting on the unorthodox place settings. She made a mental note, knowing most adults automatically corrected such oversights, unconsciously chipping away at the child's self-esteem.

Absently counting the plates, she was surprised to see five. "Are you expecting company?"

"I wasn't exactly *expecting* you," Luke replied.

"Oh, but I'm not here to eat breakfast."

"You're here. It's breakfast time. Don't fight the inevitable."

She curled her fingers a bit more tightly around the mug as her discomfort rose. Then she glanced at the children who had stopped what they were doing to stare at her.

Realizing they needed reassurance, she smiled warmly at them. "I usually only have coffee. This will be a treat."

Luke met her gaze briefly, then turned his attention back to the eggs, spooning the fluffy yellow mounds into a bowl. A moment later he glanced up at Brian. "That toast coming along okay?"

Brian carefully buttered one last piece. "Uh-huh."

"Then let's eat."

Kealey watched their interaction closely. Even for a single night's stay she had to be certain what type of home the children were in.

It didn't take long for the kids to assemble at the

table. They ate rapidly as though afraid that the food might disappear before they finished. With equal speed they reached for seconds, filling their plates. Knowing their mother had been dead for a while, it stood to reason that the children had gone hungry, that they were afraid of doing so again. Still, Kealey couldn't prevent her distressed reaction.

But Luke didn't seem perturbed by their behavior. His even, accepting manner kept the atmosphere light. She wondered if he fully appreciated the desperateness of their situation.

When the children were finally sated, Luke instructed them in clearing the table and helping with the dishes. She had to admit that he was pretty good at handling the kids.

Brian held up the freshly washed frying pan. "Where does this go?"

Luke pointed to a rack on one wall. "Anywhere you can find an empty hook."

Kealey stacked the dried dishes in a cabinet that was too high for Hannah to reach. Somehow, Luke had managed to include all of them in the task.

He surveyed the kitchen. "Okay, great job, guys. Now, upstairs, brush your teeth."

The children obeyed without protest.

Once they were alone in the room, Kealey focused again on her morning's mission. "When I spoke with Rachel yesterday, she mentioned your keeping the children for a few days. However, there's no need for you to do so. We have adequate foster homes already in the system.''

"They're comfortable here,'' Luke responded easily. "And as of last night I have beds, clothes, toothbrushes...everything they need. And it won't be for long. You should be able to locate some relatives soon.''

But she didn't return his nonchalance. ''You don't seem to understand that we have procedures to follow. They're not stray puppies.''

Something in his eyes hardened. ''I'm not suggesting they are. But I talked to Rachel, too. And I've put in an official request to keep the children until their relatives are located.''

Kealey felt some of her control evaporating. It wasn't a feeling she welcomed. ''I don't have that request in my file.''

"I filled out the paperwork last night and Rachel took it with her. She said she'd give it to you this morning.''

"I came here before going into the office.''

He shrugged. ''That explains it. I'm sure Rachel will give you the paperwork when she sees you.''

Kealey firmed her shoulders. ''I hate to be obstinate, but you seem to be forgetting that *I'm* the caseworker and it's up to me to decide where it's best to place the children. And I'm not convinced that's with you. You're a single man. And I believe children are best served in a two-parent family.''

Luke met her eyes, his own gaze probing. "Is this because of our disastrous date?"

Nonplussed, she stared back at him. "Of—of course not!"

"I'd hate to think that you'd take out your resentment on innocent children."

"Resentment?" Kealey sputtered. "What makes you think I gave our date a second thought?"

"Then why uproot the kids? They've lost their mother, been terrified they would be separated. Now they've finally slept safely in real beds without their stomachs growling in hunger. I may not have the perfect two-parent home, but it's a decent one. And I think the kids will be better off with someone they've begun to trust. More important, I can guarantee they won't be split up. Can you?"

Kealey wanted to insist that she could do just that. But she couldn't. "*If* I let them stay, and that's a big if, I'll need certain assurances." His eyes again met hers and she fought the squiggle of unease his gaze caused.

"Sounds reasonable."

"I want to be certain they won't be left alone while you're at work."

"Since my clinic's in the house that won't be a problem."

Kealey frowned. "I don't believe you can operate on animals and chase kids at the same time."

He grinned, that appealing smile she hadn't forgotten. "True. But they'll be at school a good part of the day, and I have a full-time assistant. Between us, we can keep the kids in line.''

"And if you can't?"

"If there's a conflict, I can call in the reinforcements. You forget, I've got more relatives than Campbell's has soups.''

"Still, I will be conducting frequent inspections. Despite your opinion of me, my only concern is the children's welfare.''

His easy expression faded. "You're so sure of my opinion?''

She faltered. But only for a moment. Then her professional expression was back in place. ''I'll get back to you after I've read your paperwork.''

Luke nodded.

She picked up her briefcase. Starting to turn away, Kealey was surprised when he took her arm.

"When you're making your final decision, will you remember one thing?''

Cautiously, she nodded.

The deep blue of his eyes darkened to near black. And somewhere deep inside, she felt an irrepressible shiver take hold.

"Just remember, Kealey, that the children *want* to be here.''

For a moment she couldn't reply...and she couldn't move. Snapping herself out of her paralyzed state, Kealey clutched her purse closer. "Fine." She started to step away, but then realized he was still holding her arm. For a moment she simply stared.

Then he dropped his hand. "Thanks, Kealey."

Why did his voice have to sound so husky, almost intimate? Swallowing, Kealey nodded stiffly. Then she nearly sprinted to the door. She didn't even care at that point if he knew she felt the need to escape.

"BUT WHY do we hafta go to school?" Hannah asked for the fourth time.

"Because that's what kids do," Luke explained, trying unsuccessfully to smooth her long blond hair into braids. Mary had washed the child's hair the first night, carefully combing out all the tangles. Looking up, he met Hannah's eyes in the mirror. "You've had a few days to get settled, but you're not on vacation."

"We didn't get to start school 'cause Mama died," Troy told him in a matter-of-fact voice.

"That's okay. You haven't missed too much," Luke replied.

"Can't we stay here with you?" Hannah pleaded.

"And give up recess?" Luke asked in a reasonably horrified tone.

Hannah and Troy both giggled.

But Brian wasn't convinced. "I wanna stay here."

"Away from your brother and sister?" Luke questioned mildly.

Conflicted, Brian's brows drew together. "I guess not."

Luke managed to fasten a rubber band around Hannah's crooked braids. "We'd better hustle, guys, or we'll be late."

Luke had shifted appointments and called on an associate to handle any emergencies so that the entire morning was clear. After collecting lunches, Luke gave them each milk money and then they piled into his SUV. Glancing at their freshly scrubbed faces, he could see the apprehension that new clothes and full stomachs couldn't abate.

And he understood how they felt. No one enjoyed being the new kid. Brian, Hannah and Troy had attended an elementary school on the other side of town when their mother had been alive. But they had been transported along with their mother to the hospital close to Luke's home when she'd fallen ill. Which was how they'd come to be at the grocery store in his neighborhood. It was only a few blocks from the hospital they'd run away from after their mother's death.

Despite their reluctance, Luke was taking the kids to the elementary school assigned in his neighborhood. Since they hadn't yet started the new school year at least they weren't being yanked from familiar classes.

Luke was convinced school, even a new one, would be good for them. Not only the benefits of learning, but also the interaction with other children their age, the distraction the entire experience would provide.

After registering the children in the office, Luke accompanied each of them to their classrooms. Brian, as he'd expected, stoically entered his.

Troy was a touch more timid, but he was soon drawn into the kindergarten play area. Although the next day he would begin the afternoon session, the principal had agreed it would be best to let him become accustomed to the new school on the first day his brother and sister were also attending.

Hannah, however, clung to Luke's hand, not willing to be left alone with the other first graders. And when she looked up at him with her huge, blue eyes his heart melted. With the teacher's consent, he took one of the short chairs to the small round table and sat next to Hannah. Aware that he looked ridiculous with his long legs jutting out and his tall body scrunched into the miniature chair, Luke winked at Hannah. A tremulous smile hovered on her lips.

The teacher began the session with practicing their printing. To Luke's relief, Hannah soon became absorbed in the task. It was obvious this was something she truly enjoyed. And when the teacher announced reading time, Hannah's eyes lit up. As the children broke into designated circles, Luke hung back, allowing her to blend in with the other kids.

After an hour, when Hannah hadn't even glanced at him, Luke felt he could slip away. But he found it was difficult to leave the school...to leave the kids.

Trying to shake off the feeling, he glanced at the cheerfully decorated halls, remembered the friendliness of the teachers, and continued to worry.

He knew these kids needed a champion. And not to be shuffled into an already overcrowded foster system. But could he be that temporary champion? And if he could, would the system allow it?

Luke glanced at his watch, calculating the number of hours until he could pick up first Brian and Hannah and then Troy. Nearing the office, he considered going inside to make sure they would call him if any of the kids couldn't cope this first day. To his surprise, Kealey Fitzpatrick was exiting as he approached.

"Kealey? What are you doing here?"

She glanced up, also surprised. "Checking on another case. How about you?"

"I wanted to make sure the kids were settled in before I left. Hannah was pretty apprehensive."

She frowned. "Aren't you jumping the gun by enrolling the kids in school?"

"In what way?"

"You haven't received approval to keep the children, even on a temporary basis."

"I thought that was pretty much a formality."

"Based on what?"

He looked into her bluish eyes, feeling his own exasperation rising. "On our discussion. You *know* they're in the best place for the time being." Then he remembered his own resolve to be diplomatic. "And I thought you'd want them in school. It's a way to ease them back into normality."

Slowly she nodded. "That's true."

He glanced at his watch. "How about getting some coffee? I've cleared most of my day and other than shopping for backpacks, I'll spend most of it waiting to pick up the kids."

She hesitated.

"No pressure, Kealey. But if we're going to be working together in the kids' interest, it wouldn't hurt to keep it friendly."

"I do have a few open hours. Rachel felt so guilty about asking for preferential treatment on your behalf that she's volunteered to take two of my other cases."

"Good. If we hurry, Carmach's might have some fresh doughnuts left."

Unexpectedly, she smiled. "Caffeine *and* empty calories?"

"Breakfast of champions," he retorted with a matching smile.

They agreed to walk the two blocks to the doughnut shop. It was a perfect summer day, one that mixed the warmth of the season with the sweet promise of approaching autumn. A light breeze skipped through some newly fallen leaves, shuffling them with the dripping shoots of late-budding trees.

"I love the fall," Kealey offered. "Even raking leaves. Silly, I suppose."

"Nothing matches the smell of burning leaves," Luke mused. "Too bad we're environmentally correct and have to bag them now." He was surprised to see an unexpected vulnerability change her expression. But in the next instant it vanished and he wondered if he'd imagined the transformation.

"I haven't thought about burning leaves in years," Kealey murmured. "It does seem more memorable than stuffing them in garbage sacks."

"Funny, the world spins faster in so many ways. But the seasons still change in their own time, unrushed by frenetic human activity."

Again she looked pensive. "I suppose they do. I hadn't thought about it that way."

"We get so caught up in our schedules, there's not a lot of time to think beyond the moment."

"What about you, Luke?" she questioned. "How do you manage to stay apart from the craziness?"

Surprised, he glanced at her. "I don't always. But my occupation helps. It's difficult not to stay in the moment when you're dealing with sick or hurt animals. They have a way of bringing you back to the basics, to what matters."

She averted her face, staring ahead so as not to meet his gaze. "And what matters to you?"

Luke tried not to let his continuing surprise show. He also wanted to be honest with her. "Probably

about the same as everyone else. Family, friends...
doing a job that makes a difference.''

Kealey didn't reply, but her expression dimmed.

"How about you?" he asked, wondering why she
continued to look so pensive.

She shrugged. "Like you said, it's probably the
same for most everybody.''

Somehow, he doubted that, but they'd reached
Carmach's. Opening the door for Kealey, he followed her inside, inhaling the aroma of freshly
cooked doughnuts. "I hear those empty calories
calling.''

"You don't look as though you indulge very often," she retorted.

Nor did she. But then he didn't think of Kealey
and indulgences in the same vein. She seemed too
stiff and reserved to allow herself to revel in junk
food.

So he was surprised when she ordered two gooey
doughnuts for herself. He'd expected her to stick to
black coffee.

She glanced at him. "You *did* say you wanted to
eat here, didn't you?''

Luke smiled. "Absolutely.''

Kealey reached for her wallet.

He held up one hand in protest. "My treat.''

"But—"

"I remember, you pay your own way," he replied, referring to their only date. "But this was my
idea. Humor me.''

Looking flustered, she replaced her wallet, then accepted a mug of steaming coffee. Luke carried a tray with their doughnuts and his coffee to the table. Once settled, Kealey dug into her selection.

When she finally looked up, Luke grinned.

Self-consciously, she dabbed at the corners of her mouth. "Am I wearing most of the filling?"

"Nope. Most women pick a meal to death like food's the enemy. You're a refreshing change."

"I suspect that's a backhanded compliment at best," Kealey retorted. "But then I'm not like most women."

"No," he admitted, realizing it was true. "You aren't."

Her eyes narrowed. "I also suspect I'd rather not know exactly what you mean by that."

"Maybe you'd be surprised."

She stopped midbite, removing the doughnut and staring at him. "Does the analysis come with the doughnuts?"

He shrugged. "I think you have some preconceived notions about me. And I'm not sure whether they're specific to me, or just to men in general. Either way, I don't want them to get in the way when dealing with the kids."

Something flashed in her eyes, something reminiscent of hurt, but surely he was mistaken.

"I don't allow my personal feelings to sway my judgment in regard to the children," she told him quietly.

He leaned forward, seeming to unsettle her with his proximity. "They're great kids, Kealey. Scared, orphaned and uncertain, for sure. But I'd like to do something about that—I mean until some family member is found."

She met his gaze, searching. After several seconds had passed, she picked up her napkin, dabbing at the frosting on her lips. "Then I suppose you'd better buy those backpacks."

For a moment Luke simply stared, wondering if he'd heard correctly. "Does this mean I have temporary custody?"

She sighed. "For a smart man, you're being a little thick today."

He felt the grin that split his face. Leaning even closer, he reached forward, grasping her shoulders. "I could kiss you!"

Startled, her eyes widened.

Releasing his grasp, he leaned back. "Sorry. Guess my enthusiasm got the best of me."

Kealey nodded, but her formal, professional demeanor was firmly back in place. "That's all right. But you need to understand that this situation is strictly temporary. Either the children's relatives will be located within a short time or they will be placed in a two-parent home. And that's something I *won't* budge on."

Meeting her gaze, he realized just how set she was on those conditions. Which meant he had two options. Resign himself to the inevitable, or win

Kealey over. He picked up his coffee mug, meeting her gaze with a noncommittal one of his own. Resignation wasn't part of his makeup. Now, he just had to learn what made Kealey tick. And that talent was one he possessed.

CHAPTER THREE

KEALEY WASN'T CERTAIN how Luke had talked her into going shopping with him. Yet they were standing in front of the display of backpacks, discussing their merits.

"This looks like a good standard style," Luke mused, pointing to one. "And it's roomy enough for Brian who'll probably have more to carry."

He picked up a navy-colored one. "This comes in both large and small versions. That way no one can disagree over the style. I could get them in different colors so they won't get mixed up."

"Hmm," she responded, her eyes on a girlish, pink model.

"Don't you agree?"

Kealey held up the one she'd been eyeing. "Well, actually, I think Hannah might prefer something like this. It's probably closer to the kind the girls carry."

He studied it. "Do you think she'll really care?"

Kealey's throat tightened, remembering how desperately she had wanted to fit in with the other girls when she'd been growing up, how impossible that had been. Her clothes and accessories had screamed *outsider* as clearly as a label would have.

Luke reached for the pink backpack, then met her gaze. "If you think she'd like this one, we'll get it. Now, what about Troy?"

Amazed that he'd so willingly accepted her advice, she felt an unexpected warming, a rush of appreciation for a man so tuned in to children.

Together they located a backpack emblazoned with a cartoon-character for the youngest child.

Luke held up the two smaller backpacks. "I have to admit you're right. The kids will like these much better than the plain variety." Then he glanced at the sturdy, but unimaginative one he'd selected for the oldest child. "Now, we have to find another for Brian as well."

She smiled. "Since you were able to deal with the pink, girly model, I don't think you'll have too much trouble with one for Brian."

He winced. "I guess I thought that since I have such a big family this stuff would come naturally. But I see the benefits of the female influence."

She kept her smile benign. "Luckily, you have lots of sisters."

He rolled his eyes. "With too many instructions."

"Even Rachel?"

"She's not so bad," he admitted. "Since we're younger, we both got the brunt of our older sisters' bossiness so we kind of stuck together."

Kealey managed a smile, envying his easy sense of family, the solid reassurance that never failed. A few bossy siblings sounded like a blessing. But Luke wouldn't understand that. "So you and Rachel are allies?"

Smiling, he nodded. "Absolutely. How about you? Do you have a special brother or sister?"

Kealey shook her head at the question, having learned long ago how to reply to such questions without revealing her feelings. At the same time, she knew the conversation was becoming too personal and she needed to put immediate distance between them. And she was fairly certain Luke would be difficult to dissuade. "That's my pager."

Distracted, he glanced at her purse. "I didn't hear anything."

"It vibrates," she fibbed. "Looks like you're finished here and I've got to get back to work."

"But—"

"You've made some great choices. I'll be in touch within a short time."

"Kealey, you don't have to—"

"Bye," she called back, escaping. Glancing back briefly, she saw him standing there staring, his arms filled with backpacks.

It was her own fault, she realized. She shouldn't have gotten into such a revealing conversation with him. Of course it would lead to questions. And he wouldn't understand the answers. Worse, despite years of counseling that had supposedly taught her how to deal with her past, she couldn't bear to share it.

THE FIRE ROARED, not a timid pile of skinny sticks, but huge, dry logs that crackled and warmed. It was one of the advantages of Luke's old Victorian house. The fireplaces were enormous—immense grand spaces intended to heat the home. Not that it got terribly cold in their part of Texas, but the Victorians hadn't done anything by halves.

"We built a good fire, huh, Luke?" Brian asked.

"Yep." He grinned, thinking he would be up late making sure it was out. But the kids had loved building the fire and he hated to spoil their fun.

"We never had a fireplace," Troy told him.

"Lots of people don't," Luke replied. "This house is so old, it was built before central heating."

"I like your house," Hannah said softly. "It's like dress up and make-believe."

Oh, this child was a charmer, Luke realized. They all were.

The doorbell rang, breaking their quiet circle.

Opening the door, he was surprised to find Kealey. It was the first time he'd seen her since she had vanished so abruptly in the store. "Hello."

"Luke," she replied, gripping her purse tightly.

He opened the door wider. "Come on in."

Leading the way into the living room, he glanced back, noting the apprehension on her face. Grimly he wondered if she had bad news.

But when she entered the room, her face softened. "What a magnificent fire."

"One of the advantages of an old, drafty house."

Luke's dogs greeted her with wet noses and wagging tails. Some of her stiffness evaporated as she petted them, returning their affectionate greetings.

The children spotted Kealey just then, however. While Troy and Hannah remained relaxed, Brian's smile fled, replaced by wariness.

She glanced at Luke, then back at the children. "Hi! I'm here to see how you're getting along at the new school."

"It's okay," Brian replied, not surrendering any of his trepidation.

"I like it," Hannah announced. "I got new crayons to put in my backpack."

Luke took Kealey's elbow. "Let's sit down."

Since the children were grouped into a semicircle in front of the fire, he and Kealey sat on the couch angled close to them. His cats were splayed out across the top of the cushioned back, regally surveying the visitor.

"So, tell me about your classes and your teachers," Kealey began.

With a long-suffering expression, Brian answered for them all. "It's sort of like our old school. But the stuff we're learning in my class seems kind of different."

"Has it been difficult for you to catch on?" Kealey asked.

"Nah. Luke's been helping me."

Kealey's gaze flickered toward Luke before veering back to Brian. "How about your teacher? Do you like her?"

"Yeah."

"What about the other kids in the class?" Kealey prodded.

"They're okay, too."

Since it was evident he was going to remain taciturn, Kealey turned to Troy. He was much more forthcoming, chattering about the toys and crafts in kindergarten. As the youngest, he seemed remarkably well-adjusted, obviously trusting his older siblings.

Finally she turned to Hannah. "And how's the first grade?"

Hannah bit her lip, her already large eyes seeming huge. "I was scared at first."

Kealey leaned forward. "How about now?"

"Not so much anymore. Luke went to school with me three times."

Kealey glanced at him in surprise.

He shrugged, looking a bit sheepish. "They kicked me out because I was too big for the chairs."

Hannah and Troy giggled madly. Even Brian snickered.

Kealey turned back to Hannah. "So now it's okay?"

The little girl bobbed her head up and down. "Uh-huh. They liked Luke and my backpack."

Surprise took over Kealey for a moment. "They did?"

"Mine's prettiest. I love pink."

Kealey was immensely grateful that she'd insisted on the girlish backpack. It was a little thing to be sure, but she remembered how much the little things had mattered. "I'm glad, Hannah."

Hannah blinked her cornflower-blue eyes. "Luke says you picked it out."

Again surprise flitted through her. Most men would have taken credit for the act. "But it was his idea to buy the backpacks."

Hannah leaned forward, whispering. "He's nice."

Kealey couldn't resist an answering smile. But she couldn't yet agree with the child. So much was at stake here. Luke might very well be nice, but he wasn't part of a two-parent family.

"We're going to make popcorn," Troy announced.

"You can have some," Hannah offered. Then she scrunched up her small face, turning to Luke. "Can't she?"

Luke met Kealey's eyes, his own inscrutable. "Sure. We have enough popcorn for the whole neighborhood."

"But the neighborhood's not coming over," Hannah protested.

"You're absolutely right, punkin," Luke told her. Then he reached over, picking up Hannah and raising her high in the air. "But who knows how much *you're* going to eat?"

Hannah's giggles spilled into the room. Troy,

along with a more reluctant Brian, joined in as they paraded to the kitchen, followed by the dogs.

Luke was like the Pied Piper, Kealey realized, trailing more slowly. And the longer the children stayed with him, the more difficult the break would be.

Troy and Hannah collected several bowls, all mismatched, yet somehow perfect for popcorn.

"I'll grab the popper," Luke was saying. "Kealey, do you want to help Brian melt the butter?"

She blinked, realizing again that Luke had a way of including everyone. "Sure."

And within a few moments they located a pan and the butter.

"You turn the heat real low," Brian told her seriously.

"That's right. How'd you know?"

He shrugged, a forlorn gesture. "I used to help my mom when she cooked stuff."

Kealey felt his loneliness as deeply as she had once felt her own. As the oldest, Brian's loss was keener, more difficult—because he hadn't allowed himself to be a child, to simply grieve. Instead he continued watching over his siblings, taking on the responsibility of being head of the family. She made a mental note to discuss his case with her supervisor, to see if a therapist might be in order.

Soon, kernels of corn began bursting into white

clouds in the popper, each mini explosion scenting the air. And Luke brewed hot cocoa as well.

However, Kealey was surprised when he headed back toward the living room with the refreshments. "Isn't this kind of messy?" she asked, knowing little ones tended to scatter and spill.

"My entire house is for living," he replied with a shrug. "Spills and messes included."

Within a few minutes, the kids were sprawled out on the thick rug that anchored the wide-planked wooden floor. They dug into the overflowing bowls of popcorn and sipped cocoa from steaming stoneware mugs.

Kealey perched stiffly on the couch, watching.

Luke placed a mug in her hands, then dropped down on the floor beside her, managing to share the rug with the children, yet not making Kealey feel isolated from the cozy group.

However, his proximity made her very aware of his tall, strong frame, the slant of his handsome profile. Kealey had been highly aware of his rugged good looks when they'd first met. Despite that, she was uncomfortable with someone so open, so...

So much what she wanted to be but wasn't.

Kealey had known from the moment Rachel had insisted on setting up the meeting that it wouldn't work. But Rachel was one of her rare friends and it had been impossible to refuse.

Luke turned just then, scattering her thoughts. "How's the cocoa?"

Realizing she hadn't yet tasted it, she sipped some, surprised at the rich taste. "It's better than I expected," she admitted.

"It was one of my grandmother's specials—all of us learned how to make it. And homemade has its advantages."

Looking down into his warm, unshifting eyes she had to agree. "I'm sure it does."

Hannah rose to her knees, balancing one of the bowls of popcorn. "Do you want some?" Her small fingers, slippery with butter, were having trouble hanging on to the large bowl.

As Kealey could have predicted, the bowl slid from Hannah's hands, tumbling on to the rug, scattering popcorn in every direction.

"Uh-oh!" Hannah exclaimed, her eyes widening. She looked at Luke as though expecting a rebuke.

But his calm demeanor didn't change. "Won't take a minute to clean up. I'll help." And he did, his big hands scooping up the popcorn far more rapidly than Hannah's tiny hands could do on their own.

Kealey wondered if his unflappable reaction was for her benefit. It wouldn't be the first time she'd seen a prospective foster parent fake a performance.

Luke rose when all the spilled popcorn had been picked up. "Come on, Hannah. We'd better wash those hands and get a fresh bowl. This time we won't fill it quite so full."

She scampered behind him toward the kitchen.

When Luke and Hannah disappeared from her line of vision, Kealey turned, noticing that the two boys were staring at her.

She smiled, directing her words to both boys. "Do you like staying here with Luke?"

Brian immediately looked wary. "It's okay."

Realizing they wouldn't respond to the usual questions, she changed tactics. "Did you have any pets at home?"

Surprised, Brian stared for a moment. "We had a hamster, but he died. We were gonna get a dog when we moved to a house."

"You can't have dogs in an apartment," Troy explained.

"I know. They need yards," Kealey replied. "That's why I don't have a dog."

Brian drew his brows together. "Really?"

"That, and I live alone and work long hours. That wouldn't be fair to a dog."

"That's what Mama said," Troy told her.

Kealey's heart ached for these children who had so clearly loved their mother. "Then she must have been a very wise woman."

"She was the best," Brian replied fiercely.

"I'm sure she was," Kealey said, knowing it probably was true. Also knowing how vulnerable the children were without a mother's protection.

"We like Luke's dogs," Troy told her, dividing his attention between her and the golden retriever. "Bentley got left without a home just like us."

"He did?"

"Somebody dumped him out in a field when he was little," Brian explained. "And he was real sick 'cause he hadn't had nothing to eat."

Just like these children, Kealey realized with a pang.

"But he's all better now," Troy told her. "Except for one leg that got broke when he got hit by a car."

"Luke did surgery on him," Brian offered. "He's okay except he can't run a long ways."

"Bentley probably likes being close to home anyway," Kealey responded, touched by their story—and even more by the image of a strong Luke rescuing a forgotten puppy.

"That's how Luke got Spencer and Kate, too," Troy told her, referring to the cats. "They didn't have a home neither."

"And Miles and Ginger," Brian added.

So many orphans under one roof, Kealey realized. All except Luke himself. Which was why she had run so fast the first time they'd met.

"Fresh bowl of popcorn," Luke announced as he returned to the room, with Hannah close behind him. "Did I miss anything?"

Kealey shook her head, unwilling to talk about what she and the children had just shared. Luke's kindness had affected her too much and she didn't want him to know it. Meeting Luke's far too beguiling gaze, she realized she couldn't make that mistake again.

LUKE SWUNG AROUND the rink, gaining speed on his in-line skates as he neared the turn. Brian, Troy and Hannah had eagerly jumped on his idea to go skating. It was something they'd done before losing their mother. And Luke wanted to inject as much normality as possible into their lives.

And he had to admit that he loved skating as well. He often took to the streets on his skates, enjoying the workout, the speed and the exhilaration. But he thought the controlled environment at the rink was safer for the children. No rough spots to cross or potholes to avoid.

Since it was Saturday afternoon, the rink was crowded. Luckily his last appointment had been just after noon. Wayne was still at the clinic, closing up. His assistant had volunteered, knowing the kids needed the excursion. A single man, Wayne was devoted to the animals in his care. He also had a huge soft spot for children.

Keeping an eye on Brian, Hannah and Troy, Luke allowed them some distance to interact with the other kids. It was important for them to make friends, to be drawn into a world other than that of adults. They'd had too many serious responsibilities lately. It was time for some fun.

Luke glanced up, surprised to see Kealey hovering near the rails. He wondered if their fun was about to end. It wasn't that she was a bad person, she was just so uptight. If he hadn't been accustomed to being badgered into a multitude of blind dates by Rachel, Luke would not have willingly met Kealey since she was so different from the relaxed, open women he usually dated.

Knowing it couldn't be avoided, he skated toward Kealey, coming to a tight stop directly in front of her.

Appearing startled, she stepped back.

"Looking for us?" Luke asked, noticing that the slight flush in her cheeks was rather attractive.

She cleared her throat. "Yes. Your assistant told me where to find you."

Rather than replying, he watched her, noting that doing so made her even more uncomfortable.

"Wh-which made it easy to find you," she stammered.

He took pity on her. "So, what are you doing working on a fine Saturday afternoon?"

She firmed her shoulders. "Mine isn't a nine to five, Monday through Friday job."

"I know," he replied mildly. "From Rachel."

She flushed at the reminder and again he wondered what wound her up so tightly. "I need to make my week's evaluation."

"Got any more cases after ours?"

Kealey drew her brows together, looking confused. "No. Why?"

"No reason you can't evaluate and have fun at the same time," he replied. "Let's get you some skates."

"No, really—" she began, obviously flustered.

"Won't kill you," he replied. "Not just once. And the kids will love it."

Obviously torn, she glanced toward the center of the rink where Brian, Hannah and Troy were skating along with all the other kids. "They do look like they're enjoying it."

"That's what Saturdays are for."

For a moment Kealey looked taken aback as though such a thought would never have occurred to her. Then a small smile formed on her full lips. "I suppose they are."

Luke continued watching her, wondering why he'd never noticed how appealing her mouth was.

"I won't intrude on your day," she continued. "Enjoy your skating. I can do the evaluation on Monday." With the words she started to turn away.

Uncertain why, Luke reached out to grasp her arm. "Stay."

It was only one word. One very small word. But it echoed between them.

Kealey glanced down at his hand and it made him exceedingly aware of the flesh he touched, the soft warmth of her.

She looked up, her eyes silky green. They were filled with uncertainty, something he'd never seen in her before. "I don't know how to skate."

The admission did something peculiar to his insides. Who was this superprofessional, rigid woman who had never learned to skate? Who seemed embarrassed by the confession.

Disturbed by his concern, Luke reached for her briefcase. "Let's put this in a locker."

"But—"

"I can teach you to skate."

"Really, you don't need—"

"I don't need to, Kealey. I want to."

Again flustered, she allowed him to lead the way first to the lockers and then to rent some skates.

"Let's sit down over here." Luke gestured to a bench.

But as they reached it, several kids flopped down, taking most of the space.

"You sit," Luke told Kealey. "I'll help adjust your skates."

Looking self-conscious, she slipped off slim calf-skin shoes, revealing well-manicured feet.

He couldn't stop a small smile when he saw the bright-red nail polish decorating her toes. She quickly pulled on the socks they'd purchased. Still self-conscious, she pushed one foot into the skates.

Luke reached for the bulky straps, smoothing them in place. He repeated the process with the other foot, but he found his hands lingering on her calf. Glancing up, he met her gaze, saw the trepidation in her expression. But it was mixed with something else, something he couldn't define. Her eyes had darkened, the green gliding into gray. And her mouth was slightly pursed as though in question or perhaps an interest neither of them was yet willing to acknowledge.

Slowly his hands dropped away.

Kealey seemed to hold her breath as she leaned forward slightly.

Unwilling to relinquish her gaze, he stood slowly, reaching again for her hand to help her up, as well. For an elongated moment they stood together not moving, scarcely breathing.

Then one of the kids on the bench jumped up, jostling them, and sent Kealey's untrained feet flying. Luke drew her close, steadying her.

Her face was just below his and he could see the light sprinkling of freckles on her nose, the moisture on her lips, the sooty brush of her lashes.

Kealey's mouth opened and he angled his head a bit, wanting suddenly to know the taste of her.

Then she pulled away slightly, her feet again sliding awkwardly, her laughter strained. "I can't seem to stay upright."

In an instant he pictured her lounging against him, and with a silent curse, he moved back as well. "It's just a matter of balance."

"Oh," she replied in a small, very small voice.

He cleared his throat. "Let's get off this cement and onto the rink."

She shook her head. "I don't think I'm ready for that yet."

Despite the effect her proximity had on him, he found himself laughing. "You won't learn by standing here. And you'll find it's harder to stand still than to actually skate."

Kealey was clearly doubtful. "That's hard to believe." She moved her feet a bit and started to topple.

Although she grabbed for the railing, Luke was there first, catching her. "And if you do fall, it hurts less on the wood than on cement."

"I suppose so," she replied, still looking skeptical.

He pointed at Hannah and Troy, who skated alongside Brian, all looking like mini professionals. "Don't tell me you can't keep up with kindergartners and first graders."

"Without wheels I can do just fine," she retorted, her feet slipping as he coaxed her nearer to the wooden floor.

"Just hang on to me. I don't think you can pull me down."

For a moment her face took on a satisfied bit of glee. "Don't count out the possibility."

"Why, Miss Fitzpatrick, I believe you're losing your professional demeanor."

"Think so?" she muttered, her gaze glued to her wildly skittering feet.

He laughed.

For a moment she glared at him. Then humor forced her lips upward, lifting her face into lines of laughter. In the next moment, she was veering to one side, nearly toppling again.

Still laughing, Luke caught her, and again they were face-to-face only inches apart.

Some of the laughter lingered in her eyes, he noted, while inventorying the effect of her nearness. But as he continued to hold her, it faded, replaced by a growing wariness.

"Luke!" Troy called, skidding to a near stop.

Luke glanced fondly at the youngest Baker child. "Having fun?"

Troy bobbed his head up and down, staring at Kealey. "Don't you know how to skate?"

She colored a bit, then met his gaze. "I'm afraid not."

"Don't be 'fraid," he told her nonchalantly. "I didn't used to know how to skate neither. But Brian showed me how." His eyes lit up. "And I could show you."

Luke met Kealey's hesitant eyes. "Troy and I could both help you."

"Sure," Troy readily agreed.

The youngster put out his hand, and Luke saw the change in her expression. Before he could speculate about it, she clasped Troy's hand.

Luke took her other hand, feeling her fingers stiffen within his. He leaned close, whispering so only she could hear. "You'd better let me hang on to you. I don't think Troy can keep you from crashing."

After a moment, she nodded in acknowledgment, the movement rigid and controlled.

He wanted to tell her to relax, that he was no more a threat than Troy. But the thought dwindled, replaced by a realization of another sort. Perhaps she should be wary.

Shocked by the perception, he didn't see the skaters slowing down in front of him. Even as he, Kealey and Troy crashed into the line of skaters, Luke couldn't shake that last thought. And the fact that he couldn't was more frightening than flying bodies and upended skates.

CHAPTER FOUR

AS THE OLDEST CHILD, Brian had always taken his responsibilities seriously. So when Luke had assigned the children chores, Brian was relieved. He needed to know he had a place in Luke's house and that he was contributing. His younger siblings didn't have quite the same need or understanding. However, there was no whining or complaining among them.

But it was Brian who shone under Luke's tutelage. Soon, he had learned his way around Luke's surgery and boarding areas. He had a genuine interest in the animals and they sensed it. However, Bentley was the one who adopted Brian, who decided they were a pair. The big retriever was always at his feet, shadowing the boy with uncommon devotion. And something in Brian seemed to loosen because of it.

Luke watched as the boy precisely filled water and food dishes, carefully reading the tags on each cage. It was still early in the morning, so early that they hadn't yet eaten breakfast, so early that the school bus wouldn't be by for more than an hour.

Luke would have been happy if the boy only

helped out for half an hour or so. It was what he'd expected initially. But Brian didn't seem to mind, eagerly taking on more and more responsibility.

And after the first morning, Luke hadn't had to wake the boy. Brian was up at dawn, running down the stairs to the clinic. Ignoring the lure of early-morning cartoons, he walked among the cages of the ill pets and through the kennels of those that were boarded.

And he patiently taught his younger siblings to help as well. In the afternoons, the three of them swept and hosed down the floors. They had even figured out how to work together to load the bags of food on to wheelbarrows, hauling them inside. It was heartening for Luke to see that they truly cared for the animals.

Hannah, the little mother, babied the kittens and puppies, and Troy mimicked Brian's actions, believing his older brother to be nearly perfect.

Seeing that Brian was at the last row of cages, Luke stepped forward. "How's the schnauzer?"

"Better," Brian replied seriously. "He ate more of his food."

"Water?"

"More than yesterday."

"He's a scrappy pup," Luke replied. "He'll make it."

Relief blossomed on young Brian's face, but he wasn't yet comfortable with expressing his feelings. "Good." Despite the brevity of his words, he reached to scratch Bentley's ears in a heartfelt motion. The retriever looked adoringly at the boy.

"It's easy to get attached to the animals," Luke told him casually. "I'm not supposed to since I'm the doctor, but it's there anyway."

Brian studied him. "What if they die?"

"I know I can't save them all, even though I try my best. A doctor's supposed to remain detached but I became a vet because I love animals, so it saddens me to lose one."

"But most of 'em get better, don't they?"

Luke smiled at the touch of optimism Brian was regaining. "For the most part. Now, you'd better eat your breakfast."

A half shrug of skinny shoulders told Luke that Brian hadn't planned to take the time to eat.

Luke clapped a hand on those same shoulders, ignoring their stiffening. "Nothing special this morning—just oatmeal. Let's get washed up, then round up your brother and sister."

Brian, however, was frowning. "I didn't finish cleaning up the back."

"There were more dogs and cats to feed this morning, which took you longer. Wayne and I can clean up the kennels."

Brian's shoulders stiffened even further. "I want to earn my keep."

Luke stopped, turning Brian so that he could face him. "I'm glad you have such a strong sense of responsibility, and I really appreciate all the help you've given me. And I think it's a good idea for kids to have chores—I had plenty growing up." Luke made sure that Brian met his eyes. "But chores or no chores, you have a place with me here. That's not going to change if a few kennels don't get cleaned on time. You understand?"

Longing filled Brian's eyes and he had to bite down on his lip to keep it from trembling. Still a trace of fear lingered. "I don't want to let you down."

Luke grasped Brian's shoulder, giving him a re-assuring squeeze. "That's not going to happen."

Together, they headed back to the kitchen. Brian spent more time with Bentley than usual and Luke suspected the boy was experiencing a slew of un-settled emotions. Still, it was soon time to get the kids off to school.

Hannah couldn't find one of her shoes, and Troy insisted that he bring one of the hamsters for show-and-tell. The hamster, however, had different ideas as soon as Troy opened the cage door. And fifteen minutes later, they had just located both the shoe and the pet. Even so, they weren't in time for the bus.

Leaving Wayne in charge of the clinic, Luke bun-dled the kids into his Bronco. It didn't take long to reach the elementary school. As Luke turned into the driveway he noticed a banner hanging across the doorway: Soccer Tryouts, Grades 3-6, 4:00 p.m.

"What about that, Brian?" Luke asked, pointing to the sign.

Brian shrugged. "They try out when I'm doing my chores."

Luke tapped the ballcap Brian was wearing, one Luke had purchased when Brian had eyed it yearningly. "There's no set time for chores."

"But—"

"Let me worry about the grown-up stuff, okay, Brian? I'll be here at four."

Delight tempered with caution lit Brian's expression. "If you're sure…"

"Get going. And don't forget—four o'clock."

"I won't!" he hollered with a grin, nearly dancing up the sidewalk to the front door.

And that grin kept Luke smiling all day.

KEALEY SEARCHED the field, easily locating the stands that were filled with parents. Junior soccer in Greenville was the equivalent of pro sports in big cities.

A tiny shack, barely larger than a telephone booth, sold cans of soda and cold treats that were stored in Igloo coolers. Kids stood in line, polishing nickels, dimes and quarters as they waited their turn. Parents chatted easily among themselves as they tolerantly watched their children run across the grassy field in the still-warm weather.

Everyone was relaxed. Except Kealey. Watching the ease of the others, she wished desperately she could be like them. But every bad memory she held manifested itself in tightly wound nerves. Once she had been able to relax. But that was before she'd known what was in store…the dangers that lurked everywhere once your guard was down.

A few boys skipped past her, their shouts of laughter buffeting in the gentle breeze. Every child deserved that carefree abandon—which was why Kealey had chosen her profession. If she could, she would protect every unloved and unwanted child in the world. At the least, she was fiercely determined to watch over those whose cases she'd been assigned.

Which had brought her out to the soccer field today. Scanning the crowd, she spotted Luke. Hannah and Troy were on either side of him.

Kealey made her way toward them. "Hi."

Luke looked up, his expression questioning.

"Wayne told me you were here," she explained.

"Sit down," Luke offered.

"Next to me," Hannah requested with a shy smile.

Pleased, Kealey sat on the weather-beaten bleacher. "Where's Brian?"

Hannah pointed toward the field with pride. "He's on the team!"

"That's great," Kealey replied, meeting Luke's gaze over the child's head.

"Seems if you sign up, you're automatically on the team," Luke told her.

"I see." She glanced down at Hannah and Troy. "Would you mind if they had a treat?"

"Nope. What's a game without refreshments?"

Kealey dug into her purse, unearthing quarters for them both.

"I can do that," Luke protested.

"It's my pleasure."

"Thanks!" both kids sang out, already jumping up, then running toward the refreshment shack.

"Trying to get me alone?" Luke asked wryly.

But she wasn't smiling. "It's going to make it more difficult when the kids have to leave if they become too deeply involved."

"It's junior soccer, not adoption."

"Still…"

"Kealey, kids need to feel a part of things, even if it's not permanent."

A flash of remembered pain struck her with unexpected force. "Of course, but—"

"Don't make more of it than is necessary. It hasn't been that long since these kids saw their mother die, fled the authorities and lived in a deserted alley. They need some normality. And that means school and soccer and ice cream cones."

Kealey swallowed, remembering how she'd once desperately yearned for just that.

Luke met her strained gaze, his own questioning.

Abruptly, she moved to stand.

"Wait. Don't you want to see Brian's game?"

Her throat worked. It would be wonderful to pretend even for an hour that she was part of a normal family, one that participated in soccer games, barbecues and picnics. But she couldn't allow herself that delusion. "I have a lot of paperwork to do."

"You don't want to disappoint Brian, do you?"

"Of course not, but—"

"Then stay. Nobody's ever reached the end of their life wishing they'd spent more time doing paperwork."

An unexpected smile tugged at her lips. "I don't suppose they have." She glanced toward the field. Brian spotted her just then and she waved. He hesitated but finally his arm came up in an uncertain wave.

And in that moment she knew she had to stay. More than that, she wanted to.

To her relief, Luke didn't make a big deal out of her decision. Instead, he glanced over at Hannah and Troy, still standing in line. "How about a Coke?"

"Excuse me?"

"Something to drink." He glanced at her quizzically. "How long have you been in Texas? Down here every kind of soda is called a Coke."

"Oh, right." She had moved around so much in her life that she had no particular culture to call her own. And her social interaction since she'd moved to Greenville had been nearly absent. Only his sister, Rachel, had become a friend. And that was just because Rachel had pushed and pushed until Kealey had given up in defeat.

"If you're lucky, there might be a Dr Pepper left, too," Luke told her.

Feeling his gaze lingering too long in question, she managed the noncommittal smile she'd perfected years earlier. "Great."

Together they walked toward the refreshment stand. Hannah and Troy were just unwrapping bright-red ice pops.

"Are they good?" Kealey asked, enjoying the look of pure satisfaction on their faces.

"Yum," Troy replied.

"They're the best," Hannah added.

"The owner of the local ice-cream stand makes them," Luke explained. "It's an old family recipe, but I think there's Jell-O in the mixture to make it richer. Nothing commercial can touch 'em."

Kealey suddenly had a longing to try one. "They do look good."

"Sold," Luke told her with a smile.

"Oh, a soda's fine."

"Life's not *all* about denial," he responded. "Be daring. Have one. Cherry, peach, lime or grape?"

Torn, she considered, biting down on her lower lip. "Grape," she finally decided.

He conveyed her request and his own to the teenager manning the booth, paid, then handed one to her. "And if you're a good girl, you can try another flavor later."

She removed the paper wrapper, then tasted. "This *is* good!"

Enjoying the rare treat, she smiled up at Luke. To her surprise, however, he seemed intent on watching the movement of her lips and tongue.

As suddenly, her throat dried up and her sense of speech seemed to take flight. Around them, children hollered to each other, parents chattered, and the thud of the leather ball being kicked echoed in the sunny afternoon.

Yet neither of them moved, nor looked away.

"Luke! Luke!" Troy hollered. "Look! Brian's kicking the ball!"

Luke didn't immediately look away. And when he did, he was reluctant. "Way to go, Brian!"

Hannah tugged at Kealey's shirt. "We need'a go sit in the stands so we can see Brian!"

"Yes, we do, don't we?" Concentrating on Hannah, their treats, the bleachers, anything but Luke, Kealey moved away.

The teams of third and fourth graders were nudged into place by the coaches and assistants—clearly volunteer parents. A few seemed to settle in naturally, probably veterans of past seasons. Others looked as though they'd been plopped onto foreign perches. But they all seemed to share the same enthusiasm.

Once back at the bleachers, Troy settled next to Luke and Hannah beside Kealey, situating the two adults together. Kealey deliberately chose to watch Brian, rather than Luke.

When she did, Kealey found herself growing curiously involved in the game, jumping to cheer when Brian first made contact with the ball, then traveled down the field. Excited, she turned to Luke. "Isn't that rare? Getting to play forward when you're new to the team?"

Luke smiled indulgently. "They're all new to the team. But, yes, it's a big deal."

Concentrating on Brian, she nodded. At her side, Hannah cheered for her brother. Kealey's attention was distracted from the field when Troy jumped up onto the wooden bench to holler his encouragement. Checking to make sure the child didn't topple over, Kealey glanced at Luke. He was mesmerized by Brian's performance, sheer pride oozing from every pore. But it was the look in his eyes that arrested her attention. It was affection so sharp it bordered on parental.

Swallowing deeply, she realized he was feeling like more than a temporary custodian. And that wasn't good for either him or the children. Because they needed to be in a two-parent home, not with a single man who thought treats solved children's problems.

LUKE WATCHED Troy's and Hannah's small hands carefully. Each was petting one of the stray cats he'd taken in. It was necessary for the cats to interact with humans so that the animals didn't become wild. Luke didn't want Hannah and Troy to get scratched, though. But unlike most younger children, they were gentle and took to the task naturally.

Although it wasn't officially part of his animal hospital, Luke dedicated a portion of his clinic to strays. Some came in injured, others were simply homeless. He'd garnered a reputation in town as the vet to come to if you found an animal needing help. And there was something about Luke himself that seemed to attract strays.

When he'd chosen veterinary school, his father had questioned whether the decision was due to choice or simply a way to care for all his strays.

But Luke's vocation was an extension of himself. It was as natural as the way he combed his hair, played with his multitude of nieces and nephews, and religiously followed the Dallas Cowboys. He'd never had a second thought about choosing veterinary medicine.

"Luke," Hannah spoke, still petting a large tabby. "I think Miss Tansy needs to play with us more."

Luke couldn't repress his smile. "She does?"

Hannah nodded seriously. "I think Kate and Spencer would like her."

"And you have three dogs," Troy pointed out. "So you really should have three cats."

"I should?" Luke replied, sounding entirely serious.

"Then they'd be even," Hannah added hopefully.

"But what if we find another stray dog? Does that

mean we couldn't take him in because they wouldn't be even?''

Hannah and Troy looked horrified at the prospect. But then Hannah gazed longingly at Miss Tansy.

Knowing he was doomed, Luke reached out to pat Hannah's shoulder. "Here's the deal. We'll bring Miss Tansy into the house. If she gets along with all the other pets, cats *and* dogs, she can stay."

"She'll be good!" Hannah promised excitedly.

Brian, trailed by the ever faithful Bentley, approached. "Luke, we're almost out of the food for old dogs."

"Canine senior," Luke repeated. "I'll make sure we have some on order." He had two older dogs in with his strays. Knowing it was unlikely he would find homes for them, he expected them to be permanent boarders. Luke had constructed large covered kennels in the backyard with a huge running area when he'd built his clinic. It had come in handy over the years for all the strays.

Hearing a quiet knock on the frame of the open door, Luke glanced up. It was early for a patient, but he'd come to accept that nothing about his practice was predictable.

Still, he was surprised to see Kealey peeking around the door, her expression hesitant.

"Come in," he greeted her. "Just watch your step."

Kealey glanced at the orderly stacks of pet food

and supplies on the shelves. Then she gazed at the tangle of cats on the cement floor.

"Is this the cat section?" she asked.

"It's an area I keep for strays," Luke explained. "But the dogs are out in their run. Doesn't always work to put the cats and dogs together," he added with a grin.

"Sometimes they don't like each other," Troy explained.

"I see," Kealey replied in a tone that suggested she hadn't heard this fact before.

"But the dogs and cats that live in Luke's house like each other," Hannah elaborated.

"So they do," Kealey replied, sitting beside Hannah on a scarred, but serviceable bench. "And who's this?" she asked, tentatively petting the tabby.

"Miss Tansy. She's going to come live in the house." Hannah glanced sideways at Luke. "*If* she behaves herself."

Kealey met Luke's gaze. "I see."

Displeased by the unspoken disapproval in her expression, Luke turned to the kids. "Okay, guys. Time to get ready for school."

"But—" Hannah started.

"Now," Luke told her without raising his voice.

The quiet command was sufficient. Hannah and Troy scampered to obey.

Luke picked up a towel, wiping his hands. "What's up?"

"Luke, I know you're trying to do what you think is best for the kids."

"That's an ominous beginning. What's the 'but'?"

"I'm afraid you're all growing too close."

He frowned. "You don't *want* them to feel at home with me?"

She leaned forward earnestly. "That's just the problem. They're *too* much at home with you."

He grew still. "Have you come to take them away?"

"Not today." She hesitated, not quite meeting his gaze. "But I have filed a recommendation with the court that they be placed in a two-parent home."

Luke kept a check on his temper. "*Before* it can be determined if they have any relatives they could be placed with?"

She nodded. "It's nothing personal, Luke. But I know beyond a shadow of a doubt that *every* child deserves a two-parent home. And if they're placed in a foster home with two parents, they have a greater chance of establishing a bond, one that could lead to adoption."

"So, even though they're coming to feel safe here, that they're finally having a chance to adapt to the loss of their mother, you want to uproot them?"

"As I said, Luke, it's nothing personal."

Anger pushed past reason. "The hell it's not, Kealey. Why don't you just admit it? It's personal. And it's because you haven't forgotten one very forgettable date. Don't try telling me it's because of the kids. You don't know a damn thing about kids being alone, crying themselves to sleep because they want a mother who's never coming back, and hanging on to a few bedraggled pets because they're all orphans. Do what you have to do, Kealey. But don't lie to yourself. You can't possibly know how these kids feel.'' He met her gaze, his own filled with disdain. ''Or, what they want.''

CHAPTER FIVE

THAT'S WHERE Luke was wrong, Kealey thought, as she drove away from his house. Because she knew exactly what orphans wanted. Worse, she knew exactly how they felt.

It wasn't a terribly extraordinary story. She was only one of hundreds of thousands of foster children. When she was five years old her mother, Frannie, had taken her to the toy store and left her in an aisle filled with dolls of all sorts. Anxiously, Frannie had made Kealey promise she wouldn't leave, that she would stay in the same spot. Frannie had also promised she would return.

Hours later, Kealey remained on her ordered spot, forlorn, tired and hungry. But her mother wasn't back. Finally noticed by both patrons and store clerks, the authorities were called.

The initial assumption was that her mother had been in an accident. It was even whisperingly considered that she'd met her death. But neither the hospitals nor the morgue had held Kealey's mother. Frannie Fitzpatrick had simply disappeared. A single mother who barely remembered the man whose brief affair had produced young Kealey, Frannie couldn't deal with the responsibilities of motherhood. It was fun she craved, not family.

For months, even after she'd been placed in a children's home, Kealey believed her mother would return. She imagined that her mother had been in a terrible accident and couldn't remember her name. But she also believed that once her memory returned, her mother would rush to her and take her home.

When Kealey had arrived at her first foster home, she'd been greeted by a well-meaning guardian. The woman, upon hearing Kealey's story, promised her that her mother would return, that her faith would be rewarded. Elderly and kind, the woman didn't realize that second promise was nearly as damaging as the first. And then, the woman fell ill, and Kealey was yanked from her home.

The next home wasn't nearly as kind. The woman used foster children as a personal workforce. And after Kealey broke her arm falling from a fence she was painting, the woman simply cursed and traded her in for an uninjured child.

But Kealey thought the accident was a miracle when Lisa, a young, exuberant woman, became her next foster parent. It seemed an idyllic situation. Lisa was filled with energy and promises. And the one Kealey took to heart was that Lisa was to be her new mother.

Kealey, at that point still able to believe in promises, fully believed that she was destined to stay with

Lisa forever. And then Lisa met Vance. He was handsome, successful and willing to marry Lisa. But he wasn't willing to take on a foster child. Lisa made all sorts of excuses to Kealey, along with even more promises that she didn't keep. But the result was the same.

Abandoned and unwanted. That summed up Kealey's existence. But she still had her dreams. In those she was adopted by a loving two-parent family. And, despite numerous disappointments, abuse and an enduring disenchantment, she still believed that was the ideal for every child. It was what she fought for on behalf of each child she represented. And it wasn't an ideal she was prepared to abdicate.

Not even to Luke Duncan.

Despite the uncertainty he created within her, she had to think of the children first. Even though she was tempted to slam on the brakes, turn around and explain, Kealey knew she couldn't. It simply wasn't in her. The ability to share her feelings, really any of herself, had been stolen along with her trust.

There were times when Kealey fantasized about being open, able to trust. But it was nothing more than that. People like her couldn't hope to have what Luke Duncan took for granted.

Biting down on her lower lip, Kealey accelerated, leaving Luke Duncan behind. And hoping to outrun her own demons.

ANGRILY, Luke slammed one of the back doors in the clinic. The children had left for school some time ago. And Wayne didn't poke his nose in where he was pretty certain he wasn't wanted. In Luke's opinion, it was one of his assistant's finest qualities.

But slamming the door did little to relieve Luke's anger, even though it had been two hours since Kealey left. Continuing to stew, he made himself calm down as he walked into the animal treatment area. They always had a relaxing effect on him.

The phone rang, the sound only adding to his annoyance. "Yes?"

"Good morning to you, too," Rachel greeted him.

He put the phone away from his mouth, sighed, then tried not to sound antagonistic. "Sorry. I haven't had the greatest morning."

"So I hear."

Immediately on guard, he increased the pressure of his fingers on the receiver. "That so?"

"What'd you do to Kealey?"

"What'd *I* do?"

"I really don't want to turn this into a marathon inquisition. I simply need to get to the crux of the problem."

"Then why don't you ask your *friend?*"

Rachel's patience evaporated completely. "Look, you nitwit, if you want to keep those kids even a day longer, you'd better learn how to behave."

"That's not the problem, Rach. She's determined

to yank them away. I could recite poetry standing on my head and it wouldn't impress her.''

Unexpectedly Rachel laughed. "I'd pay to see that."

But Luke couldn't be humored. "Don't you think I'm doing a good job with these kids?"

Rachel hesitated, her social worker persona kicking in. "Well, I suppose so."

"You know damn well I am. But that's not enough for your pal. She plans to put them in the first two-parent foster home she finds."

"Well, that *is* the ideal situation."

"Depends on the two people, doesn't it?"

Rachel's pause was telling. "Well, of course, but Kealey's only following our guidelines."

"I've heard you talk about your cases in the past, Rachel. You've placed children in one-parent foster homes a lot of times because they're better than the two-parent ones."

"Perhaps. But with Kealey it's a real cause. I'm sure she won't remove the children unless she's certain she has an equally qualified home to place them in."

"Why can't she just leave them alone?"

Rachel hesitated. "It's because of Joey, isn't it? Luke, not all foster homes are like his. I wish you could forget—"

"Forget that one of your friends was taken away from his parents because his dad was an alcoholic? And that his foster parents abused him so badly that he never walked right again? Or maybe I should forget that they messed up his mind so much that he's still in a state hospital?''

"Luke," Rachel pleaded. "Don't torture yourself. Joey's the exception."

"Then why did you become a social worker, Rach? To save kids like Joey, if I remember right."

Anguish colored Rachel's voice. "I know. But I don't believe Kealey would ever, ever let that happen to one of the kids in her care. The papers she filed today are a recommendation that will apply more to an adoption situation than a foster one."

"Can you guarantee that?"

Again Rachel hesitated.

"I didn't think so."

"Luke, you're still just thinking temporary guardianship, aren't you?"

"Sure. Why?"

"I wondered if you were thinking about something more permanent…because of Joey."

"If I ever decided to adopt a child, Rach, it'd be because I love the kid, want to be his father, not because of guilt."

She hesitated.

"What now?"

"Don't you see, Luke? The longer you keep these kids, you're more likely to fall in love with them."

"It's a chance I'll risk. I'm not going to let them be separated right now just to spare my feelings. Once they're placed in a permanent home, I'll get over it. Hell, they might find a relative tomorrow. What kind of person would I be if I let my own concerns outweigh those of these kids?''

''You wouldn't be Luke Duncan,'' she replied in a resigned, but loving tone. ''Just try not to get too attached, okay? Kealey's not going to relent.''

''She's something else,'' he retorted, still not completely mollified.

''You have to understand that you need to work *with* Kealey, not against her if you want any chance of keeping the kids on a temporary basis. Aggravating her only harms your position.''

''She was born aggravated,'' Luke retorted.

''In that case,'' Rachel replied mildly, ''you have even more reason to stop lighting her fuse.''

''You know I hate it when you're right.''

Rachel's tone turned smugly cheerful. ''It's a character flaw of yours.''

''Don't you have some work you should be doing?''

''Yes, but you're not on my agenda today.''

Luke chuckled. ''Point taken.''

''Then get to work. And I don't mean on your patients.''

As he hung up the phone, Luke realized he should have come to the same conclusion Rachel had on his own. He probably would have in time.

And the truth was, he owed Kealey an apology whether she was the kids' caseworker or not. He'd been rude. They might not have had a magical beginning, but that didn't give him the right to throw it back in her face. Sighing, he realized he had some fence-mending to do. He just wished he'd thought of it before Rachel had.

KEALEY WAS EXHAUSTED. It had been a long day. Made longer because of the relentless memories she couldn't quash. But she'd done her best, pouring all her energy into one of her cases. It was a heart-breaker. A child, abandoned by her parents, then taken in temporarily by an aunt and uncle. They were the only relatives in the family who had even considered giving her a home. All the others had refused outright. And when they'd agreed, Kealey had high hopes that the move would be permanent.

But the couple had decided the little girl was more work than they wanted to take on. And she wasn't an unusually troublesome child. She was simply an energetic six-year-old. And she'd cried huge gulping sobs when Kealey had driven her to the children's home. No explanation could soothe or make the child understand why not one person wanted her.

Feeling empty and powerless, Kealey climbed from her car. Neither the prospect of an empty house nor a frozen TV dinner appealed to her.

She trudged up the sidewalk, turning at the brick half wall that led to her apartment. Then shock held her in place. Luke, Hannah, Brian and Troy were grouped around her front door.

Immediately, her damaged spirits sank even farther. Had Luke decided he, too, had had enough of foster children? It wouldn't be the first time a foster parent had dumped children on her without notice. It *was* the first time it had happened at her home. But then Luke had probably wheedled her address from an unsuspecting Rachel.

Hannah rushed toward Kealey. "We thought you'd *never* get here!" the little girl told her with a huge smile.

Kealey sent a questioning, almost censorious gaze at Luke.

"We're gonna have a picnic!" Troy announced, having run up to her as well.

"A picnic?" she asked numbly. "It's almost dark." But her words were simply a mask. What were Luke's intentions? Was this his way of cutting the ties with the children? Of choosing to return them to the system? Had her insistence that they be placed in a two-parent family come to this?

But his gaze was easy and casual. "What? No adventure in your soul? Who says picnics are just day-time events?"

She blinked, trying to recover. Were they really here on such an innocent mission? "I—I guess I never thought about it."

"Then start," he said with a smile that turned the order into a fun suggestion.

Kealey held up her briefcase. "I just got home from work—"

"Which is why I came by instead of calling," he

interceded. "I convinced Rachel we had only honorable intentions so she'd give me your address. Hope that was okay."

She nodded numbly.

"It was for expediency. After you change clothes we can be on our way in minutes."

Kealey wanted to point out that perhaps she had a social life, maybe even a date, that she wasn't available on a moment's notice, but much of her defiance had been sapped that day. So much so, she doubted she had the energy for anything other than falling into a chair. "It's very kind of you to include me in your plans," she said, directing her words to the kids. "But I've had a really tiring day."

"All the more reason to relax now," Luke told her, obviously not prepared to relent.

"You four can have a great picnic," she insisted.

"But we want *you*," Hannah said, her big blue eyes pleading.

A touch of Kealey's impotence faded. Perhaps this was one request she *could* grant. "It'll take me a few minutes to change."

"We'll wait," Hannah told her happily.

The child's smile brought a lump to Kealey's throat, as she remembered the other little girl's hopeless sobs. She turned to fit the key in the door, her hand shaking. Then Luke's hand was over hers, unlocking the door, pushing it open. He held her back for a moment as the kids scooted inside.

"Is something wrong, Kealey?"

She hesitated, then shook her head. "Just a killer case. The kind you want to make all better, but you can't."

"Don't you see that all the time?" he asked, his gaze probing.

"Of course. But it never makes me immune. Each child is different, special. And each one deserves to have dreams and hopes and trust."

"And you want to give it to them?"

She laughed, a bitter aching sound. "Sounds ridiculous, I suppose. Obviously I can't save the whole world."

"No, but you can chip away at it, one child at a time."

She met his gaze, his words touching her already oversensitized emotions. It seemed as if, for just that moment, he read her heart. Again, she swallowed the lump of choking feelings gathered in her throat.

But he didn't say anything else. Instead he reached for her briefcase, carrying it as he shepherded her into the apartment ahead of him.

"There should be some sodas in the fridge," she began vaguely, looking around as though not certain which way to turn.

"Why don't you go change into something comfortable? I'll make sure the kids don't get into any mischief."

Still distracted, she nodded. "I'll just be a minute."

She disappeared behind one of the white doors in

the hallway and Luke glanced around at the apartment. He was struck by its complete lack of character. White walls, beige carpet, beige furniture. It appeared to be a furnished rental.

Strolling deeper into the living room, he was startled to see there were no family photos in sight. Perhaps she kept them all in her bedroom. Still, it was startling that nothing revealing the real Kealey Fitzpatrick was on display.

He entered the kitchen to make sure the kids were behaving. The room was sparkling clean and tidy, but once again without character. He opened the refrigerator and found one neat six-pack of soda. And it was accompanied by only one small carton of milk, three apples and an orange. He didn't open the freezer, but guessed it held little more. In fact, the entire apartment looked as though a solitary suitcase could be packed, leaving behind no clues as to who the occupant had been.

"Okay, guys, let's sit down at the table and make sure we don't spill the drinks."

They obliged, and a few minutes later, Kealey appeared in the doorway of the kitchen, looking self-conscious.

Luke's gaze traveled over her slim figure, now encased by jeans and a cotton shirt. It was such a drastic departure from her usual stiff suits that he was taken aback. Even on their date she'd worn one of her nondescript, conservative suits.

Kealey clasped and unclasped her hands, then fiddled with her belt. "Is this okay?"

Okay and then some in Luke's estimation. Belatedly, he cleared his throat. "It's perfect."

Kealey smiled at the kids. "Sorry I don't have much to offer you." She walked over to one of the cabinets. "I don't think there's much to snack on."

"That's okay," Troy replied. "We're gonna have a picnic, 'member?"

"How could I forget?"

"Are you ready?" Hannah asked, bouncing a bit in her chair.

Luke cautioned her with a look, but Kealey chuckled. "I believe I am. How about you?"

"We've been ready *forever*," Hannah replied.

"Not quite that long," Luke told her, ruffling the child's hair. "But now we can get going."

Hannah, along with her brothers, leaped up from the table.

As Luke stood, he caught Kealey's gaze. "You'll find they're great at taking your mind off your troubles."

"Yeah. I imagine they're pretty great all round."

He smiled thoughtfully. "I think so."

She nodded, then hesitated. However, the children were out of earshot. "I'm not sure why you're including me in this picnic."

"Any reason not to?"

She opened her mouth, but no rational answer came to mind. "You just surprised me."

"And sometimes, Kealey Fitzpatrick, you surprise me."

Not sure how to reply, she allowed herself to be ushered out with the kids. Once in the car, the kids grew more excited, giggling every time the picnic was mentioned.

When they arrived at his house, Luke shut down the engine and a new wave of giggles erupted. Kealey glanced at him suspiciously. "Is there more to this picnic than you're telling me?"

He looked appropriately insulted. "Such as?"

Again at a loss for words, she climbed out of the vehicle.

Twilight encircled the faded Victorian home, softening its already charming lines.

Welcoming lamplight flowed out the expansive bay window near the front door.

The children skipped ahead, leaving the door open. Luke took her elbow. "I think their excitement's outweighing their manners."

"It's okay," she managed to say, distracted by the feel of his hand on her arm. "They're just being children."

"Too many people today think children ought to be miniadults. When I was kid, my parents didn't demand that, but a lot of my friends expect their kids to spout the classics by first grade and then be bionically attached to a computer before they're out of diapers. Whatever happened to childhood?"

Kealey swallowed a boulder-size lump of memories. "Not everyone gets a Rockwell upbringing."

"Agreed. But too many adults forget about imagination, make-believe, that sort of thing."

"Make-believe," Kealey murmured. She hadn't thought about that since her third foster home.

"I happen to think it's one of the ingredients that adds up to a healthy kid. My family wasn't wealthy—and it's expensive raising that many kids. But we had plenty of what really mattered." He laughed suddenly. "And with the eight of us, probably more than our share of aggravation for my parents. But they never let it show."

She pressed her lips in a thin line, wishing, regretting. "That's great."

"And we grew into fairly respectable human beings without the pressure most kids today get." When she didn't reply immediately, he nudged her gently. "Going to give me an argument about the respectable adult part?"

But her voice was soft, not argumentative. "You and Rachel are the only members of your family I know, but you both seem to be decent, well-rounded people."

His gaze sharpened and she glanced away, unable to bear his probing look.

"Kealey?"

But she still couldn't meet his gaze. "Okay, so where's this picnic you promised?"

He led her through the house, but when they

reached the French doors that led into the backyard, he took her hand.

She looked at him in question.

"Sorry. You have to close your eyes. The kids insist on a complete surprise."

For a moment she couldn't release his gaze, wishing just for a moment that she was an average, untroubled woman standing beside this unusually handsome man, planning to spend a romantic night together.

It was more in defense than agreement that she closed her eyes. Placing what little trust she possessed in him, she allowed Luke to lead her over the uneven grass of the backyard. Stumbling a bit, she felt him steady her. Her mouth dried at his touch, but then he took away his hands.

"Open!"

For a moment, stunned surprise kept her silent.

The kids, however, wouldn't allow the quiet to linger. Hannah clapped her hands together. "What do you think?"

"It's—it's marvelous!" Kealey replied in a wondering voice. And it was. The aged gazebo that stood in the corner of Luke's sprawling yard was set for a picnic. A checkered tablecloth covered the wooden floor and five plastic plates and silverware were grouped in a circle. A vase of handpicked flowers decorated the center. Old barn lanterns hung from the rafters and gables. Each was lit, casting soft light over the structure.

"I lit the lamps," Brian told her proudly.

The gesture showed trust, Kealey realized. But then Brian seemed to be proving he was worthy of the confidence Luke placed in him. "They're perfect."

Brian smiled, glancing at Luke for confirmation.

A thumbs-up gesture from Luke broadened his smile.

Two coolers sat beside the gazebo. "One's for hot food and the other's for cold," Brian explained.

With Luke's dogs surrounding them, the kids opened the coolers, tugging out canned drinks and a few bowls. Even the cats strolled up to join the children, tails swishing in mild inquiry.

"Come sit down," Luke invited. "The kids want to serve the food." He leaned closer, lowering his voice. "They did most of the cooking."

She kept her voice low as well. "That's okay with me. I've never been a picky eater." Growing up, she'd never had a choice. And it had never occurred to her to indulge her tastes now that she was an adult.

Luke's smile was teasingly wicked. "Good."

The kids quickly arranged the serving bowls, a basket of hard rolls, and the drinks.

Troy proudly handed Kealey one of the smaller bowls. "It's 'paste' salad. *Ladies* really like it."

Managing not to smile at his unintentionally humorous words, she met Luke's gaze, before turning back to Troy. "You're right. It's my favorite." She took an extralarge helping of the shrimp pasta salad. "Umm."

"We made beanie weinies and macaroni and cheese, too," Brian told her.

"I like them as well," Kealey replied, taking generous portions of both.

When the kids were involved with their own food, Luke leaned closer. "You're being a good sport."

"So are you," she whispered back. "I love *paste* salad."

For the first time, they shared a genuine smile. Kealey tried to return her attention to the meal. But Luke was too compelling, too captivating.

Up this close, she could see the faint lines near his eyes etched by a lifetime of laughter. Somehow, she knew this with a certainty. Because he was a man of laughter, of good, easy times, a man carved from a lifetime of care and love. Kealey didn't know how she could be so sure of him, but she was. And that certainty unnerved her. Had she been wrong about him? About his ability to keep and nurture these children? About her own unsettling attraction to him?

The blue of his eyes darkened. Could blue turn to black? she wondered vaguely. And were men allowed to have such thick, dark lashes?

"We have ice cream, too," Troy announced.

His words drew Kealey out of her trance. "Oh, good. I like ice cream."

"After dinner," Luke cautioned.

"Okay," Troy agreed. "But there's chocolate *and* strawberry."

Kealey couldn't resist one more glance at Luke. "That *is* something to look forward to."

"I like chocolate," Hannah confided.

"Me, too," Kealey admitted. "But sometimes it's fun to have both. Then it tastes like chocolate-covered strawberries."

The kids looked intrigued.

"I can guess which flavors they're going to pick," Luke told her.

Kealey's eyes widened. "Oh, I'm sorry I suggested it. I hope you don't mind."

His face screwed into a question mark. "Why would I care?"

"Of course. Why?" she repeated, trying to disguise her misspoken remark.

"Luke lets us help pick the groceries," Brian told her. "Then we make up what we want for dinner."

"Really?"

"Within certain guidelines," Luke responded. "As long as we get in protein, vegetables, fruits and some dairy, I figure we're doing okay."

She relaxed, trying to forget she always had to be on guard. Glancing around at the healthy kids, she relented. "Looks like it's working."

"I know how to make tuna noodles," Brian told her. "My mom showed me how."

"She was a smart woman," Kealey acknowledged. "Every man should know how to cook and keep house."

"Keeps us men out of the clutches of scheming women," Luke told him with an exaggerated wink.

Brian snickered.

But Kealey couldn't take offense when Luke so clearly was teasing. Instead she turned to Hannah. "That's okay, sweetie. They'll come crawling when they realize we can make brownies and they can't."

Luke sighed soulfully at Troy and Brian. "Take heart, boys. It only gets worse."

"Really?" Brian asked.

"Afraid so," Luke replied. "But they're so cute and pretty, it takes the sting out of the whole process."

Despite her best intentions, Kealey blushed. Not that she really thought Luke was referring to her. It was just so unexpectedly sweet. So incredibly, surprisingly sweet.

To distract attention from the telling flush, she smoothed back Hannah's golden hair. "Yep. Who could resist this face?"

Luke glanced from Hannah to Kealey. "Not me."

The beginnings of starlight stabbed through the lattice awning of the gazebo. Or maybe it was moonlight, Kealey thought irrationally. Didn't someone once say that the moon cast more than mere light on young lovers? The whimsy struck her forcefully. And, unaccustomed to whimsy of any sort, she was helpless to resist the feeling.

CHAPTER SIX

RACHEL ADDED another pink packet of artificial sweetener to her iced tea, the spoon swirling lazily, occasionally clinking against the tall clear glass.

The noise didn't bother Kealey, but the delaying tactic did. "You going to tell me why we're eating lunch today?"

Rachel continued stirring. "It is a daily event as I recall." Finally she laid the spoon down on a paper napkin. "And we have had lunch together before, you know."

"True," Kealey admitted. It had only been occasionally, though. Between their busy work schedules and Kealey's reluctance to encourage closeness, it wasn't something they did often. "Somehow, I feel you have a particular reason today."

Rachel nodded. "Actually, I'm feeling guilty about giving your home address to Luke. I completely trust my brother, but..."

Kealey took pity on her. "Like you, I don't think Luke would ever do anything inappropriate with the information."

A trace of guilt still shadowed Rachel's eyes. "But it's against the rules. And I'd be the first person to object if someone released personal information about me. Which makes me feel pretty hypocritical.''

Realizing the depth of Rachel's remorse, Kealey met her gaze. ''Rachel, you'd never do anything to harm a co-worker, a child in your care or frankly anyone else. Luke's quite persuasive.'' Kealey remembered the touch of his hand on her arm, her own uncharacteristic weakness. ''And he truly did only want to surprise me.''

''Was it nice?'' Rachel asked hopefully.

''More than nice,'' Kealey remembered with a wondering smile. ''He and the kids planned an evening picnic and it was...''

''Yes?'' Rachel prompted.

''Sweet,'' Kealey managed to say finally, trying not to sound dreamy. ''Really, really sweet.''

Rachel's eyebrows rose in surprise. ''I have to say I'm rather amazed.''

Suspicion born of experience slithered close. ''You are?''

''Just that Luke's notoriously laid-back. I've never seen him go to much trouble for the women he knows. Not that he's a cad, or anything like that. Just that he kind of goes along with things rather than planning anything out of the ordinary.''

Pleasure was pushing aside suspicion. ''Really?''

Rachel's gaze turned speculative. ''But then I don't think I've ever really seen Luke really fall for a woman. He's had zillions of dates, a few semi-serious girlfriends, but not the big one.''

Embarrassed, Kealey waved away the words. ''Don't be ridiculous. This is just business.''

''Uh-huh. I know I conduct most of my casework beneath the stars while sharing supper.''

''It was because of the kids!'' Kealey protested, realizing it was true. ''Luke said it was their idea.''

''Without the least bit of guidance from him?'' Rachel questioned skeptically.

''Well, I'm sure he helped with the food.''

Rachel rolled her eyes. ''I don't know which one of you is denser. But okay, we'll play it your way. You had a moonlit picnic, courtesy of the kids. Does this mean you two are getting on a bit better?''

For a moment Kealey was nonplussed. Had the entire picnic simply been engineered to sway her decision?

Rachel continued speaking, cutting into those thoughts. ''When I spoke to Luke I realized he was feeling a little guilty about being short with you the other morning. Like any male, he blurts out the first thing on his mind, then begins to realize it might not have been too kind.''

''Oh,'' Kealey murmured, still wondering about Luke's motives.

''And the absolute truth is that at heart Luke's just a big softie. He can bark pretty loudly at times when he's defending what he believes in, but he wouldn't purposely hurt anyone. Why do you suppose the man has more strays than any veterinarian within two hundred miles? He just can't say no. Pretty soon, he's going to run out of room to keep them all.''

The last of Kealey's suspicions dissipated. ''Well, don't some of them, I mean...''

''Luke has a flat, no-kill policy. He tries to find homes for them, but that's a full-time job on its own. So, he keeps feeding and caring for them, and every once in a while one gets placed in a home. And, of course, the whole family has at least one pet courtesy of Luke.''

Kealey was overcome. ''But he can't save every stray in the world!'' Then it struck her. Could she and Luke possibly share this flaw? The desire to somehow save every child and stray animal they could?

''Maybe not. But he's been trying to since he was about five years old. He brought home every wounded bird, raccoon and rabbit that got hurt in the fields. And you wouldn't believe how many dogs and cats we had.''

''Didn't your parents mind?'' Kealey asked, fascinated in spite of herself.

Rachel laughed. ''I guess with eight kids, a few dozen animals isn't as daunting as you might think. And they seemed to sense from the start that there was something special about Luke, something in him that needed to rescue and help. And not just animals, he brought home every outsider in school who needed a little attention, even just a decent meal. That's just Luke.''

Kealey considered this. ''You're lucky your parents were so tolerant.''

Rachel nodded. ''They've always been great. Never complained about Luke's menagerie. I just hope he doesn't find himself having a problem with the huge brood he has now. He has a special license because he's a vet, but I understand a few of the neighbors have complained. Luckily, even though it's not a main artery, his street is a mix of residential and commercial. Otherwise…''

''Hmmm.''

''You have that 'we've got to find a way to fix this' look on your face, Kealey. But we've got enough kids to deal with, without taking on animals, too.''

''You're right,'' she murmured in agreement, still thinking.

Rachel groaned. ''I can see I shouldn't have told you.''

Kealey smiled at last. ''You *have* been revealing quite a bit lately.''

Rachel grimaced. ''So I have. I just hope this wasn't one too many.''

IT WAS A regular checkup. And it was a regular Wednesday afternoon. But it had been several days since Kealey had seen Luke and she was unreasonably nervous.

Wayne had told her that Luke and the kids were back in the boarding area. By now, Kealey knew her way around the clinic well enough to find it on her own.

She could have predicted the scene. Hannah and Troy sat amid a swarm of cats, enjoying the animals as much as the cats enjoyed the attention.

Brian, with Bentley at his side, was checking tags on all the cages.

Luke spotted her first. His eyes lightened, not a huge change, rather a shift so subtle it was barely perceptible. Yet it warmed her more than such mild interest should. "Hey, Kealey."

"Hi," the children chorused only a moment later, noticing her after Luke spoke.

Hannah, despite her enchantment with her feline friends, ran toward Kealey. "We're doing our cat job!"

"And you've got lots of cats to work on," Kealey acknowledged, dropping one hand on Hannah's shoulder. "Aren't there a few more than just last week?"

"Seven more," Troy told her.

"We inherited an entire family," Luke explained. "The owner decided to get rid of the mother and her complete litter. Didn't want any more kittens. Unfortunately, they didn't even consider spaying her."

"That's so they won't have more babies," Hannah whispered to Kealey.

Kealey hid her grin as her gaze collided with Luke's.

"They're working with the animals." His brows lifted. "A few nature lessons are bound to come their way."

She tempered her grin. "Are you going to have room for all the new additions?"

"We'll have to," Luke replied.

"Until we can find homes for them," Brian told her.

"Any luck with that?" Kealey asked.

"Uh-uh. We tried but we don't know any people who want 'em. Nobody we asked took one."

Kealey had been thinking about the problem since she and Rachel had discussed Luke's growing brood of strays. "Is that the difficult part? Matching people with the pets?"

"You've pretty much hit it on the head," Luke confirmed. "I know there are probably people who would be a perfect fit with the strays, but it's a lot easier to find the animals than the people."

Kealey took a deep breath, uncertain how her idea would be received. "How about having a doggy and kitty adoption party?"

Luke stared at her in silence and she immediately felt like a fool. The man had been taking care of strays all his life. Why had she thought she could fix the problem without an iota of experience?

"A party?" Brian asked, obviously intrigued.

"Could we come?" Troy asked.

Kealey's lids sank shut. Luke was going to want to throttle her.

"I never thought of that," Luke was musing. "You mean like with refreshments and balloons and music?"

"Well…I guess," she replied, stunned that he was actually considering her idea.

"And we could wear hats!" Hannah crowed.

"So could the dogs and cats!" Troy agreed.

"Well, maybe bandannas," Luke suggested. "They might not like hats."

"Miss Tansy would," Hannah bragged.

"I thought you wanted to keep her," Luke murmured.

Horrified, Hannah shook her head. "You said—"

"Don't panic, little one. Just pointing out you don't want to dress her up too much, otherwise she could be irresistible." He glanced up as he spoke, catching Kealey's gaze.

Unexpectedly, irrationally, she wondered at the undertone of his words.

Relieved, Hannah agreed. "But people could see how nice she is and want to adopt another kitty."

"How will we get people to come to the party?" Brian asked.

"I've been thinking about that," Kealey replied. "We can put flyers in stores and restaurants, and tack them up on telephone poles. I'm sure we can put an item about it in the paper. And the local radio

and TV channels would probably announce it on
their community bulletin board segments.''

Luke looked impressed. ''You *have* given this
some thought.''

She flushed. ''I figured you were going to run out
of room pretty soon.''

''When are we going to have the party?'' Brian
asked.

Luke's expression grew thoughtful. ''I guess we
could do it the Saturday after next.'' He glanced at
Kealey. ''If that's enough time to do the flyers and
publicity?''

''I think so. I know the community bulletin board
coordinators from working with them at the agency.
The flyers and newspaper should be a cinch.''

''Then it's set,'' Luke decided, his gaze turning
to include the kids. ''That's means our prospective
adoptees will all need baths.''

For a moment Troy looked dismayed. Then he
brightened. ''Oh, you mean the dogs and cats!''

Luke chuckled. ''I didn't mean you guys. But the
cats will probably just need a good brushing.
They're not too fond of baths.''

''We can do that!'' Brian offered eagerly.

''Yeah!'' Hannah added.

''Great idea, Kealey,'' Luke said with a smile.
Then he lowered his voice so that it only reached
her. ''And now you'll have to let the kids stay with
me at least another week and a half. You wouldn't

set them up with a party and then not let them come, would you?''

Dismayed, Kealey realized she'd been so caught up in the preparations for the party that she hadn't considered the consequences. Luke was right. It would be incredibly cruel to involve the children in the planning and then deny them the event.

And meeting Luke's gaze she couldn't miss the gleam that said he knew he was right. Worse, that she was aware of it.

LUKE SAT TENSELY in one of the few adult-size chairs in the elementary school's office. Amazing how easy it was to feel like Gulliver with all the miniature furniture and accoutrements around you.

It was Luke's first parent-teacher conference. And he hadn't realized how nervous it would make him. As he stared at the principal's door, it seemed the letters grew larger, almost looming.

A soft touch on his arm nearly made him bolt.

"Luke, is something wrong?" Kealey asked in concern.

"No—no, of course not."

But she didn't look convinced. "Are you worried about what the principal will say?"

"Not really." Then he wiped sweaty hands against his trousers. "I never did anything like this before."

Kealey's eyes softened. "I'm sure they're just going to tell us how the kids are interacting with others, maybe give us a preview of their grades.''

Luke met her gaze. ''You think I'm nuts, don't you?'' He rose, unable to stay still. ''It's just that I've been entrusted with a lot and I don't want to let the kids down. I think I've made sure they've done their homework, tried to help them fit in, but you never know, do you? I could have done something wrong, something—''

''Luke!'' She rose, grasping his arm. ''As far as I can tell, you've done everything right.'' Her gaze caught his. ''The fact that you're so worried is incredibly touching. But I think you can relax and simply be happy about what you've accomplished.''

His gaze for once was neither soothing nor amused. ''You mean that?''

She could have stayed within the official guidelines and remained neutral. But somehow she just couldn't. Raw, honest emotion deserved the truth. ''Yes, Luke, I do.''

He picked up her hand, the motion as simple as her words.

And she couldn't have drawn it away if she'd wanted to.

Only moments passed before the outer door opened again. Unobtrusively, Kealey withdrew her hand. And in short time, the conference began.

It didn't take long to learn that each child's teacher had only praise for the children's schoolwork and behavior. Soon Luke's apprehension gave way to pride.

The principal stood at the conclusion of the meeting and extended his hand. "You can be very proud of these children, Mr. Duncan. Your devotion to them shows."

"They deserve the credit," Luke replied. "They're great kids."

Staying behind, Kealey collected the necessary notes for her files. When she exited the office, she spotted Luke leaning against the wall, obviously waiting for her.

She'd assumed he'd left and couldn't repress a spurt of pleasure that he hadn't. She held up the folder. "Got what I needed."

His gaze lingered over hers. "So did I."

She looked at him questioningly.

"Thanks for keeping me from falling apart."

"You wouldn't have. You'd have handled it on your own just fine."

"Yeah. But it's nicer when you don't have to."

So it was, Kealey realized. But she still couldn't admit that to Luke. She glanced at her watch. "I'm running late."

The change in his expression was subtle, yet she caught the gleam in his eyes that said he knew she was escaping. That only made her want to run faster.

"Don't forget!" Luke called out as she headed toward the door.

For a moment she paused, then tried to think. "What?"

His expression segued into knowing resignation. "The pet adoption party on Saturday."

"I *did* get all the advertising together, so I should remember the date."

His full lips edged upward. "Yeah, but you've got that look on your face that says you've eliminated every thought or action not connected to work."

Not every single one. Not the ones connected to Luke Duncan, the ones that remembered the touch of his hand, the gaze she couldn't forget. "I have a busy job. It takes a lot of concentration. But that doesn't mean I'll forget about the placement party."

His partial grin grew, and her stomach struggled to keep pace. "So you'll be there."

"Of course."

His gaze was unsettling. "Good. Otherwise we'd miss you."

She nodded, awkwardly turning back to the door, rapidly replaying his words. He'd said "we," hadn't he? Not the kids would miss her, or even more specifically, Hannah, since she'd formed the closest bond with Kealey.

No, he'd said "we." *We.* It was such a small word, one most people peppered their conversations with. But then Kealey wasn't most people. And right now, *we* sounded like the warmest word she'd ever heard.

CHAPTER SEVEN

THERE WERE AT LEAST a million reasons why Kealey could have avoided the party—tons of paperwork that she could never catch up on, a pile of laundry that was screaming for attention, and then, of course, her own dislike of social situations.

But there were three more inescapably compelling reasons to attend. Hannah, Troy and Brian.

While Kealey had initially been surprised at how well the children had taken to Luke's strays, now she was overwhelmed by their total and selfless devotion to them. She knew most kids would have contrived dozens of excuses to avoid the work. But the Baker trio acted as though the animal-related chores were a reward. Orphans helping orphans.

Kealey looked upward, frowning as she spotted a few grayish clouds scuttling across the sky. The one thing that could ruin their outdoor party would be the weather.

Parking several houses away from Luke's, she noted that the street was already filling up. Grabbing two bouquets of balloons, she glanced at her watch, seeing that she was thirty minutes early, in plenty of time to help decorate.

Bypassing the front door, she opened the arched wooden gate that led to the backyard. Surprise held her still. Seemingly dozens of people roamed through the yard. Some were attaching bouquets of balloons to rafters, others were draping streamers, and even more were filling long banquet-size tables with food.

As she stared, someone coughed behind her. She turned and met a smiling male face.

"Excuse me, ma'am, we need to bring the canopy through here and set it up," the good-looking man told her.

"Sure, didn't mean to block the way," she explained, scooting to one side.

"We're just the troops," a second man explained. "Luke's the commandant and he'll have our skins if we don't get this tent thing up in time."

"Oh," she responded, guessing the canopy was Luke's way of guaranteeing dry weather even if nature didn't cooperate.

As she ducked out of the way, several women scurried by and Kealey vaguely recognized Luke's sister, Mary. Shrinking back against the spiked boards of the fence, Kealey watched the pandemonium with a sort of horrified amusement. Surely all these people weren't Luke's relatives.

Just then Ruth turned around, her face brightening as she rushed in Kealey's direction. "Hi! I thought that was you! It's great seeing you again."

"You, too," Kealey replied politely.

"Have you met everyone?" Ruth was asking. "The two nimrods trying to put up the canopy are our brothers Mark and Matt."

The two men, wearing welcoming smiles, waved bits of canvas in her direction.

Mary spotted her as well, hollering out a welcome. "Hey, Kealey!"

At the identification, a horde of people converged on Kealey.

She wondered if this was how the quarterback felt when the opposing team's defense attacked. Smiling, she hoped her trepidation wasn't visible.

"This was all *your* idea, I hear." One man exclaimed, extending his hand. "I'm John, another brother."

"Well, I wouldn't say it was my idea—"

"That's what the kids told us!" yet another man told her. "I'm Peter."

Kealey couldn't conceal a startled glance.

But Peter along with his brothers and sisters were laughing. "You guessed it. Matthew, Mark, Luke, John and Peter. Mother and Dad aren't religious nuts. I think they hoped the biblical influence would have a calming effect."

Luke moved to stand beside Kealey, offering a steady presence. "Not that it worked."

"Nope, they were a bunch of heathens," an older woman told her as she joined them. Brunette, just beginning to show a few strands of gray, she was still an arrestingly attractive woman. "Probably why my parents named me Jane—no doubt as in Calamity Jane. They were wise enough to know that parental ambitions have severe limitations." Jane clasped Kealey's hands. "I'm Luke's mother, I've been so looking forward to meeting you."

Meeting parents, other than in a professional capacity, wasn't Kealey's thing. But she tried to be as friendly as the other woman. "It's nice meeting all of you as well."

"Kind of you to say so, but we can be rather overwhelming. You probably feel like the sole remaining potato chip at a picnic, with forty hands grabbing for the last bite. Why don't you leave your balloons with the boys and come over with me to the sign-up table? You can help me get it into order."

Agreeing, she walked toward the makeshift sign-up table with Jane just as Hannah, Troy and Brian tumbled outside. Shrieking in delight, Hannah sped toward Kealey and Jane, her brothers not far behind.

Kneeling down, Kealey got an extra big hug from Hannah. Then she gently tucked a wayward lock of hair behind the little girl's ear. "Looks like you guys have just about everything ready."

"I put bows on the kitties," Hannah whispered.

Kealey's smile erupted. "I see. Even the boys?"

Brian looked disgusted. "She's got junk on all of 'em."

Troy drew his brows together. "Do you think that'll make people want 'em more?"

Kealey remained diplomatic. "I'm sure the pets look wonderful with or without bows."

"We gave 'em baths," Troy announced. He held out one arm with a reddish scratch. "But Frankie didn't want one."

"Frankie?" Kealey searched her memory as she gently ran her fingers over the scratch, seeing that it wasn't serious, yet dropping a light kiss on it. "Isn't he a cat? I thought Luke told you not to bathe them."

"He was extra dirty," Brian explained.

"And we didn't want him to not get 'dopted 'cause he was stinky," Troy added.

Kealey again tried not to smile. "I see."

"And Luke says you can't put perfume on 'em," Hannah told her seriously.

Jane hid a laugh behind a cough and Kealey hugged the three Baker children in turn. "Well, you've done a stupendous job. I'm sure Luke's very proud of you."

"He says we're extra...extraorbs," Troy told her.

"Extraordinary," Kealey murmured. And so they were.

A speaker screeched just then and they all looked up.

"My grandsons—hooking up the music for the party," Jane explained.

"It looks like you have a nice group of them," Kealey replied politely.

Jane laughed. "I realize we may have more family than good sense, but I wouldn't have it any other way."

Kealey pushed the toe of her pink tennis shoe in the grass. "Is it difficult at times? I don't mean to pry—"

"You're not. Of course it's difficult. I've spent many days wondering how we'd manage. When the children were young, before Timothy got established, I worried about money for clothes, toys, medical expenses. Then, because we did have so many kids and with prices soaring, I worried about college, weddings. But it all worked out somehow. With enough love, you can accomplish anything."

Unexpectedly, tears misted Kealey's eyes at Jane's beautiful words. But she didn't allow them to fall. She was surprised the tears even threatened. Years of cultivating her hard shell had nearly obliterated the impulse. But lately her emotions seemed to be rising to the surface. "Your children are very lucky."

Jane shook her head. "No, I'm the lucky one. Nothing in the world gives you greater joy than children. And now my children are having the same experience. Finally, even Luke."

Shocked, Kealey stared at her. "But that's only temporary!"

Jane's tone was quiet, gentle. "I know. But the love doesn't have to be. And that's what really counts. Of course the children need a permanent home, but I doubt they'll ever forget the care Luke's given them. And, if in the future, times aren't perfect, maybe they'll look back and remember there was one person who loved them, and did his best for them.''

Kealey's voice choked. ''What if that just makes it worse? Makes them long for what they can't have?''

Kindly, Jane linked her arm with Kealey's. ''There's no way to predict another person's memories. My kids tell me they have only wonderful memories of growing up.''

''Perhaps it's because you were a great mother.''

Jane shook her head. ''Maybe. And maybe it's what they *want* to remember. I didn't have a big family growing up. My parents died when I was eight and my grandfather raised me. He did his best, but he was at a total loss as to what to do with a little girl. I remember longing for frilly dresses, hairbows, things all the other girls had.'' She met Kealey's eyes. ''Sounds silly now, I know. I was hardly scarred by the loss of such trivialities, but somehow at the time it seemed terribly important. And that could have been my most significant childhood memory. But do you know what I remember?''

Kealey shook her head.

''I remember my grandfather reading me bedtime stories every night.'' Jane laughed softly. ''He didn't have too many children's books, so oft as not he read to me about fishing tackle or the latest tractor or thrasher on the market. But he was so careful to make certain I knew I wasn't alone. He always left the hall light on—told me it was because he couldn't see if he needed to get up at night, though I knew the truth. It was so I wouldn't be scared in the dark. And every morning, he brushed my hair, said he used to brush my grandmother's hair when she was alive. And even when his hands were so gnarled with arthritis he could barely pick up the brush, he insisted on doing it. I think it was his way of letting me know he loved me."

"That's a beautiful memory," Kealey murmured, wondering if Jane was right. Could a person pick and choose their memories, deliberately hanging on to the bad rather than the good?

"Which is what I think Luke is creating for the Baker children," Jane replied. Then her kind but probing gaze met Kealey's. "With your help, of course."

"If you mean in my official capacity—"

"Not completely. That's part of it, of course. Allowing Luke to keep them at least for now. But, more importantly, your part in helping them believe in themselves."

"I don't understand—"

"You suggested this party. It's giving the children the opportunity to help other orphans. True they're canine and feline orphans, but still, it makes the kids feel important, that they're doing something that counts."

Touched both by her words and her innate kindness, Kealey didn't know how to respond.

But that didn't seem to faze Jane, either. "You're helping to give them hope, Kealey."

"What if we can't follow through on this, what if we've given them false hope? Doesn't that frighten you?" Kealey asked in a worried voice.

But Jane didn't waver. "I haven't been frightened since the day my parents died. My grandfather promised I never had anything else to fear because he would always be there for me. And he was."

But so many promises had already been broken, would continue to be broken, Kealey wanted to scream.

Jane reached out and took Kealey's hand again. "Please don't worry, dear. Luke has big shoulders. I don't know if he told you this, but he was determined to work his way through college and then veterinary school. By then, Timothy was making good money and we had a decent inheritance of land that we sold for a good profit, but Luke wanted to do it on his own. I guess he thought eight college tuitions were still a stretch. He had excellent grades so he was awarded a scholarship, but it still meant long hours and a lot of hard work. At the same time, he established the first nonkill animal sanctuary in the county. He's always worked big and dreamed big. And he's brought home every wounded animal and person he's encountered."

Kealey got the feeling Jane was referring to her.

"That must have been quite a lot of extra work for you."

"Sometimes it was," Jane replied, surprising Kealey who had expected a selfless declaration. "In fact, there were times I could have conked him for wrecking a special dinner by dragging in every door-to-door salesman or missionary. And sometimes, even when you cook dinner for a family of ten, there's not enough to stretch it another half dozen ways."

"But you got a lot out of each experience?"

"No," Jane told her, again surprising Kealey. "But Luke did. I didn't realize it at the time, but those were the events that shaped him into who he is today. I wish, that as a parent, you could know automatically which things are important, which ones will matter in the long run, but it's not that easy. Sometimes you go to great lengths to plan events you think will mold character and solidify family remembrances. And later, your kids either don't remember them or didn't think they were significant. Then, there are those times when you throw something together and your kids still talk about it years later. Parenthood doesn't come with a manual, Kealey. It's instinct. You either have it or you don't. And I think Luke has it."

Biting down on her lip, Kealey had to agree. Too bad she hadn't been able to learn those instincts from a parent like Jane. And that wasn't something you could compensate for by picking up a book in the child-rearing section of the local library.

"And you have the instincts, as well," Jane continued.

Kealey jerked her chin up, shocked. "You can't possibly know that from just meeting me." Kealey swallowed her own regret. "Worse, I'm afraid you're wrong—I'm not mother material."

"Nonsense. You're a natural."

Kealey cleared her throat. "I don't mean to be disrespectful, but—"

"Kealey, being a mother isn't a definition from *Webster's*. It's about bringing out the best in kids, encouraging them in a way that teaches them. Like today. I'm not saying they'll grow up to be veterinarians or philanthropists. But just maybe, they'll grow into adults who care about others, especially those who can't help themselves."

Kealey gazed over at the Bakers. They fit in among Luke's many nieces and nephews as though they'd known them since birth. "If they do gain something like that from today, Luke gets the credit."

"I've found that credit often comes in pairs. Much like what two people bring to parenting. I was an only child—and as I've told you, one with a less than usual upbringing. But my husband, Timothy, had a huge family, ten brothers and sisters. His paternal grandparents also lived with them. I think in a lot of ways I wanted a large family more than he did. He was ready for a little peace and quiet. I was ready for what I'd never had, what I thought I'd missed."

"Do you regret having so many kids?" Kealey couldn't resist asking.

"Every time they drove me nuts," Jane replied with a laugh, "which was on a daily basis." Then her gaze softened. "And now I can't imagine a moment without them. But that's what life's about—change. From who we were to who we want to be."

"Maybe not all of us are looking for change."

"I'd say it's a good bet that none of us are. Change isn't very comfortable. I hate to even consider painting the walls a new color, but life has a way of grabbing you and making you adjust to change whether you want to or not." Jane smiled suddenly. "I was thrilled to be a mother, but I wasn't any too anxious to become a grandmother. There's something about that word—implies you're past it, one of those smudgy, gray little people who are no longer seen as women."

Kealey couldn't halt the laughter that came with Jane's unlikely description. The woman was still without a doubt madly attractive. "Smudgy?"

"You bet. It's my word and I like it. Despite my best intentions, my daughter, Mary, had her first child." Jane reached up suddenly to brush at her eyes. "I can't believe what a goon I'm being. My heavens, that was fifteen years ago."

Kealey thought Jane's reaction was terribly touching.

Jane managed to laugh. "Good thing I recovered. I've got twenty-one grandchildren now."

Kealey's voice softened unexpectedly. "I'm just amazed how you can have this incredible family and still look so young and beautiful."

Jane's gaze gentled. "Luke was right about you. You are very special."

Something deep and warm unsettled her. "He said that?"

"And more. Mothers, however, are supposed to be known for their discretion." Jane's gaze swept across the yard. "I'm afraid I'm known more for my huge brood than anything else."

"Another thing to be proud of," Kealey replied.

Again Jane smiled. "Like you."

Confused, Kealey drew her brows together. "Me?"

Jane pointed to the Baker children who were efficiently completing the setup. "Just look at them."

"But I'm not their mother."

"Incidentals."

"Hardly. Mrs. Duncan—"

"Jane."

Kealey took a deep breath. "Jane. I'm their caseworker."

"And Luke's their foster dad. But look how far the kids have come in just a short time. When I first met them, they were terrified, sad and somewhat angry. Most of all, I don't think they believed in anyone. They certainly didn't believe they'd still be together."

"But that's still not for sure."

"Granted. But I hope you'll be able to work out something. Hasn't there ever been a time in your life when you wished you could change something for the better?"

Startled, Kealey felt as though the woman could see inside her.

"This could be that time," Jane continued. "Luke's been trying, and in some part succeeding, for most of his life. But this one would mean the most."

"If he and the kids become too close, it will be wrenching for them all when they're removed from his home."

Jane's gaze settled on Luke who was lifting Troy onto his shoulders. "I'm afraid it's too late for that."

Kealey was, too. And that was the brunt of the problem. Should she rip the kids away from a safe, happy environment to protect them from further pain? Briefly closing her eyes, she remembered the few good homes she'd been placed in. If she could have stayed longer, she wasn't certain it would have hurt worse to leave. Perhaps she could have been happier longer. What was it Jane had said? That we choose the memories we hang on to.

"Kealey!" Hannah called out. "We're ready to start!"

She hesitated, but Jane smiled. "I have things here under control. I just thought you looked like you needed rescuing from the clutches of my many, many children. Go ahead."

Still thinking about Jane's words, Kealey joined Brian, Troy and Hannah. As the eldest, Brian was in charge of the kennel gates. Hannah was in charge of the candy-colored leashes she and the boys had chosen from Luke's stock. And Troy was guiding visitors toward the kennels.

Luke caught her eye and then reached her side seconds later. It seemed to her that he stood a bit closer than usual. "So, what do you think of your 'little' party idea?"

"I can't believe your whole family came out in support."

"Are you kidding? I've talked each and every one of them into adopting one or more of my strays in the past. They're just hoping to be saved from taking another cat or dog."

"Your mom's really nice," Kealey continued, realizing Jane was the kind of mother she'd always dreamed of. Kind, considerate, but with enough character to make her interesting.

"Yeah, I'm kind of fond of her," he responded. "Have you met my dad?"

"Well, no, but—"

"Might as well get it over with, Kealey. You know you'll have to meet the whole family."

"I will?" she responded weakly.

"You don't want to hurt their feelings, do you?"

"Of course not."

Luke smiled, taking her hand, tugging her across the lawn until they reached his father. "Dad, I want you to meet Kealey."

"Call me Tim." A tall, older and still handsome version of Luke greeted her with a grin. "So, you're the young lady I've heard so much about."

Unsure how to take that, she tried to smile. "You have?"

"With three daughters and four daughters-in-law, there aren't too many secrets in our family."

"Secrets?" she echoed, her discomfort level increasing with each word.

"You're the young lady who's helping Luke with those cute kids, aren't you?"

Luke draped an arm over Kealey's shoulders. "Dad, we might be coming on a little strong for Kealey. I don't know how big her family is, but I'm guessing it's nowhere near the size of our mob."

"Good point, son." Tim leaned closer to Kealey. "We can talk more later when we're not being censored. But before you go, I want to tell you this party was a great idea. Super job."

"Thank you, but—"

"Don't even try," Luke interrupted as his father lifted his brows, then winked and moved on across the yard. "It *was* your idea and my family's big on supporting each other."

"I'm not part of your family," she replied quietly.

Luke stared at her, seeing the vulnerability she usually masked. "You don't get it, do you?"

She shook her head.

"You're helping part of my family—specifically, me with the kids. To my family, that makes you part of us. Family's not about blood and genealogy, it's about caring and trusting and helping each other no matter what. Don't you imagine my brothers and sisters and their families had better things to do today than come to a pet adoption party? They're here because it's what we do. You've never told me much about your family, but I'm guessing it isn't that way."

Her expression clouded.

"I'm right, aren't I?" he persisted.

"Luke, not everybody's like your family, throwing around feelings like confetti on New Year's. Some of us are more...private."

Again he searched her eyes. "What makes you shut yourself off, to push away people when they get close?"

But she was physically backing away. "Luke, stop. I'm here to help with the party, not to be psychoanalyzed."

Realizing she might truly run away, he stopped

the inquisition. ''Why don't we give out balloons to the kids who are looking at the prospective pets?''

She blinked, then stared at him suspiciously. ''Balloons?''

''That or start passing out the punch. I've been thinking people might be more conducive to taking home one of our little adoptees if they're in a true party mood.''

''I noticed there's quite a spread on the buffet,'' Kealey mused.

''My family brought enough food to feed half the town.''

Kealey glanced at the large signs posted around the lawn, stating there would be no adoption fees. Luke had already spayed and neutered the animals. ''I was worried that the signs might not be large enough when we were making them, but they look okay.''

''The whole thing is great, Kealey. Just relax and enjoy it.''

If only it was that easy. Still, she joined him as they strolled around the yard, explaining the adoption procedure to potential owners.

The first hour they had a lot of lookers, but no takers. The kids still seemed hopeful, but Kealey was beginning to worry. What if this had been a terrible idea? What if no one adopted a single pet?

Meeting Luke's gaze, she realized she was conveying her concern when he winked and sent her an encouraging thumbs-up. Still, the next twenty minutes crawled by.

Then a young couple with a five-year-old son chose one of the smaller dogs. Paperwork complete, the dog on one of the candy-colored leashes, they left with smiles nearly as large as Brian's, Hannah's and Troy's.

A family with three little girls arrived next. The parents insisted they wanted only one kitten, one that all the girls could agree on. But each child chose a different kitten and after prolonged pleading, the parents gave in and took all three.

With four adoptions behind them, the kids were pumped.

It was nearing noon and Kealey worried that they still had a lot more strays than adopters. Then she glanced at the long table of food and inspiration struck.

Within minutes she searched for and found the leftover poster board and began lettering some new signs. Seeing what she was doing, Ruth and Mary joined her. Kealey couldn't stem her astonishment at how this family operated.

"This is a smashing idea," Mary told her, holding up one of the completed signs that read Free Lunch and Pets.

"I'm not sure it'll do any good," Kealey demurred.

"Are you kidding?" Ruth interceded. "If you weren't so good with kids, you could be in the PR

business. Luke told us how you did all the flyers
and the advertisements as well.''

Struck by the fact that Luke had complimented
her to his family, it took her a moment to reply. ''I
like kids.''

''It's obviously mutual,'' Mary told her. ''Little
Hannah can't stop talking about you.''

That warm feeling was crawling through her
again.

Rachel had joined them, and she placed a friendly
hand on Kealey's shoulder. ''You guys don't know
the half of it. Kealey's the most dedicated caseworker I've ever seen. She cares about these kids as
if each and every one were her own.''

Embarrassed and more than slightly astonished,
Kealey flushed. ''Rachel, we *all* do that.''

''I do my best, but there's something about you,
Kealey. Something that makes you connect with
them in a way I've never seen before. With you, it
seems incredibly personal.''

Mary and Ruth sat quietly, seeming to sense any
pat comments would be grossly out of place.

But Kealey was in agony—anytime someone
came this close to guessing she had a special connection to the children in her care, her reason for
choosing her job, Kealey ran. It was why she'd only
lived in Greenville a year, why she'd fled from town
to town since the beginning of her career. All the
old instincts jumped into place, even though she'd

only told Rachel that she had no family and that she'd moved around a lot.

At the same time, a new sensation coursed through her. She didn't want to run again, to sever her connection with the Baker children...or with Luke.

Rachel picked up one of the signs. "Kealey, Mary's right. These is a smashing idea! Who can resist sandwiches, cookies, puppies and kittens?"

"Perhaps we shouldn't make it sound like that's our menu," Ruth mused with a twinkling smile.

Kealey guessed that Mary and Ruth had somehow realized they were becoming too personal and were graciously backing off. While she appreciated their sensitivity, her spirits sank. If they could see her distress, she'd revealed too much.

Perhaps it *was* time to move on. Kealey had accepted long ago that, because of her background, she couldn't ever be a mother or wife.

At one time she'd entertained the notion that she could draw on her experience. Then she would remember her mother's face the day she'd been abandoned. How did she know she wouldn't repeat Frannie Fitzgerald's mistake? How could she be sure it wasn't a genetic flaw, something no amount of willpower could conquer? Nothing would make her risk the fate of the children she longed to have. As a caseworker, if she failed, another social worker could step in. But as a mother, there was no backup.

And since her birth certificate revealed a father

she'd never known, Kealey could only assume her mother had been a failure as a wife as well. And without knowing anything about the man who appeared in her life only as a neatly typed name on an official document, she didn't know what other failings she might have inherited from him as well.

Rachel and Ruth moved off with two of the completed signs.

Mary remained behind. Her voice was quiet. "I know that we often come on like gangbusters—especially since there are so many of us. But please don't think we're prying." Her kindly eyes were filled with a wisdom resembling her mother's. "When someone comes into our family, for whatever reason, we find ourselves caring for them. Though I do realize that not everybody's comfortable with what probably seems like nosiness." She cleared her throat. "But just because we dig into each other's lives, we don't do that to everyone else."

Kealey's smile was wobblier than she intended. "I didn't realize I was so transparent."

"You're not." Mary's voice continued to be gentle. "But I'm the oldest sister, and I've been a mother for a lot of years now as well. It gives you a sort of radar. Although I'm used to how the Duncans operate, I do know that's not for everyone. So don't let us scare you away."

Kealey swallowed, trying to sound level, unaffected. "I'm made of pretty tough stuff."

"I'm certain of that," Mary replied quietly. "Perhaps even tougher than you realize."

Surprise held Kealey still for a moment.

But Mary didn't let the silence grow uncomfortable. "I know you've met my five children."

Kealey nodded.

"I was convinced I could never raise one, let alone a handful."

"But you grew up in a loving, happy family!" Kealey protested.

Mary shrugged. "Sometimes that's not all there is to it. At least not for everybody."

Kealey considered these surprising words. She'd just assumed that being raised in a loving family insured you'd become a natural parent. "You overcame your concerns, though."

Mary laughed softly. "Sometimes, you just have to let go of your fears." Her glance traveled across the yard toward her husband, a man who'd begun to gray and whose waistline had also thickened. "Especially if you love someone enough." He looked up just then, his loving gaze landing on his wife.

Mary cleared her throat. "You'll have to excuse me. I'm still nuts over my guy." Then she gazed over at Luke and the kids. "Luke's a natural, though. I always thought he'd be great with about a dozen kids."

Kealey again felt uncomfortable. "You do realize

that he may not be able to keep the kids much longer.''

Mary didn't seem surprised. ''Of course. Having a sister in the foster care business has clued me in somewhat. But whether he does or not, I hope you'll know that you're always welcome here, with our family.''

Kealey blinked. ''But—''

''It's just who we are, Kealey.'' She laid a gentle hand on Kealey's outstretched arm. ''And we don't expect you to be like us.'' She smiled, a teasing gleam in her eyes. ''We like you anyway, just as you are.''

Startled, Kealey couldn't immediately reply.

Breaking into the moment, Hannah came over. ''Kealey, guess what?''

''What?''

''The signs are working! Look!'' She pointed to the trickle of people coming through the gate.

''Oh, my,'' Kealey murmured, inordinately pleased.

Hannah ran off toward the kennels and Mary stood as well, her smile at once teasing, kind and welcoming. ''I just *love* being right. It *was* a smashing idea.''

CHAPTER EIGHT

THEY WERE all exhausted. But it was a good kind of exhausted. They had found homes for two-thirds of Luke's strays. And the Duncans had remained behind to clean up and put away everything. One by one, as order was reestablished, the family members took off, until only Luke, Kealey and the kids remained.

Luke had been sure Kealey would escape as soon as possible, but she'd lingered. The expression on her face was one he hadn't seen before. She seemed somehow reflective.

Her idea for free lunch had not only brought in people who had adopted the pets, it had also wiped out all the food his family had brought over, along with everything in his kitchen.

"I definitely think it's a pizza night," Luke announced. "We have a lot to celebrate."

The kids clapped their hands.

"Let's go to Little Bit of Italy," Luke continued.

Kealey looked at him in question.

"It's the oldest and best pizza place in town. The wife of the original owner was from Italy and now it's second generation. Can't beat it."

She nodded. "I should be going anyway, let you have your dinner."

"I meant all of us," Luke replied quietly, still wondering about the softer look on her face.

"I—"

"You *have* to come," Brian told her. "You're the reason we had the party."

Looking touched, Kealey knelt beside him. "That's very sweet of you, but you and your brother and sister deserve the credit. You're the ones who cared so much about the animals and wanted to make sure they had loving homes."

"But you *will* come, won't you?" Troy asked.

Kealey glanced up at Luke. "I wouldn't miss it."

More relieved than he'd expected to be, Luke met her gaze. "Okay, troops. Out to the car."

Twilight was giving way to darkness, as they drove toward the oldest part of Greenville. The center of the little town still had an old-fashioned Main Street with buildings dating from the 1800s. The street was only five blocks long, but it held the essence of Greenville's charm.

Some of the buildings were still false fronted, a few others were constructed of brick or stone. The two-story building that housed Little Bit of Italy looked as ancient as its faded brick exterior. But it was the aged grace that made it so inviting.

Inside, old fresco walls, softened by age rather than design, truly looked as though they belonged in Tuscany rather than the wilds of Texas. Dozens of sconces held beeswax candles while a huge iron chandelier filtered muted light over the room. Framed family pictures that represented several generations were mixed among subdued, inviting oil landscapes of both Italy and Ireland.

They were greeted warmly and seated within moments among the other diners. As they accepted menus, Luke watched for Kealey's reaction.

She looked up just then. "How could I not have known about this place? It's delightful."

"I've always liked it," he agreed. "But then I'm a sucker for history. Daniel O'Brien went to Italy in World War II, fell in love with Gina Luciano, and brought her back to Greenville. Back then she must have felt as though he'd moved her to the real Old West. Legend has it he was so in love with her, he wanted to recreate a part of home for her, so he bought this old building. They moved in upstairs and remodeled this level for the restaurant."

"Sounds like a labor of love," she murmured.

"I'll say. Dan O'Brien had two left hands and was about as handy with a hammer as most people are with laser rockets."

She laughed, a soft pleasing sound. "Then how'd this come to be?"

"Dan did his best. But when he had done all he knew how to, he bartered for the rest of the work. He was an accountant and he found plenty of contractors, electricians and plumbers who needed their books put in order. Gina supervised the plaster work—wanted it to look like it did back home. Then she and Dan painted and decorated.''

Kealey glanced at the rustic, Mediterranean tables and chairs. ''I wonder where they found the furnishings.''

''They didn't. Dan found a cabinetmaker, Gina sketched the drawings, and between them, it worked. Gina and Dan wrapped the woven straw around the seats of the chairs themselves. And from what my grandparents told me, at that point, they were finally ready to open the restaurant. By then, after all that work and investment, they were terrified that little old Greenville wouldn't take to something so foreign. But the fact that it was so different was what attracted everyone.

''The O'Briens spent the last of their savings on a jukebox, which I guess was a big splurge. The fantastic food, the charm of the place, and the fact that they could dance to the music on the jukebox, well, Granddad said it was *the* Saturday night hangout.''

Kealey glanced around at the small crowd. ''Looks like it's still popular. Only in a good way. Friendly, but not too noisy or crowded.''

Luke nodded. ''It's not trying too hard.''

Kealey's gaze lightened in recognition. ''Exactly. Sometimes places like that are just plain exhausting.''

Luke realized it was one of the few glimpses he'd

had of the real Kealey. Again he wondered what it was she was so carefully preserving.

And why did it seem so important for him to find out?

The air seemed to hush as the evening progressed. The pizza arrived and the children attacked it with their usual enthusiasm, but it was Kealey who Luke continued to watch. She assisted Troy with his pizza in a way that didn't make it look as though the five-year-old really needed help. The youngest child was always wanting to act as grown-up as his older brother.

And there was a softness in Kealey's eyes and her manner as she laughed and talked with the kids. But when her gaze caught his, he could swear her bluish-gray eyes changed to the green of her cotton shirt. How could he have overlooked that before? Especially when her eyes were so compelling....

Kealey glanced up again as she picked up her glass. But she didn't take a drink. Instead her tongue nervously touched her lips as though they'd gone suddenly dry.

The children's chatter dimmed, much as the night around them had. How was it he'd never really noticed just how delicately pretty Kealey was? Probably because *delicate* never seemed to describe her before.

The old jukebox cranked out another tune, this time a slow song from the fifties, a sweet, melancholy tune. And Luke knew he wanted nothing more in that instant than to hold Kealey in his arms.

His gaze still on hers, he stood and held out his hand. "Dance?"

Although she looked startled, she nodded, a wobbly uncertain movement.

Luke was suddenly glad that the room was so small, the dance floor even smaller. With only the few other couples beside them, it seemed immensely intimate.

And then she was in his arms.

Chest to chest, their hands connected, their bodies leaning closer. Luke had a wild desire to drag her as close as physically possible, to feel her against him, if only for a fleeting moment.

But the vulnerability in her eyes stopped him. If he didn't know better, he would think it was a silent plea. Another urge possessed him, the urge to protect her, to uncover what hurt had caused this lingering doubt.

Even as those thoughts surfaced, he glimpsed something else in Kealey's expression. Mixed with her insecurity was a longing, at least he hoped it was longing.

So he drew her an inch closer.

And there was no panic in her eyes. Instead they seemed to change color again, becoming a mysterious pewter he couldn't quite read. Was that a flicker of interest that blossomed when his grip tightened?

Her eyelids drifted shut. The song's haunting melody seemed to move them even closer, until their faces were scarcely a breath apart. At this distance he could see the soft ivory of her skin, the brush of a few defiant freckles, and the fullness of her lips. Lips that seemed to be curving in invitation.

Luke was just about to accept when the song ended. With a will he hadn't known he possessed, Luke forced himself to withdraw, to glance at the children, to make sure they were okay. Absorbed in their pizza, they hadn't seemed to notice anything amiss.

Returning his gaze to Kealey he could almost say the same about her. Except there was a new flush to her cheeks and a betraying increase in her breathing that belied his first assumption.

Something stirred inside and made him want to shout. But he had a feeling she wouldn't be pleased if he did. In fact, he guessed she would probably run as fast as she could.

Which meant he was going to have to figure out how to make her stay.

KEALEY AVOIDED Luke's house for two days, but it was killing her. She wanted to see Luke, which she knew was the main reason she should stay away.

And she wanted to see the kids, not in a professional capacity, but because she found she missed them as well. How had these three crept under her skin so quickly, so surely? She'd had dozens of similar cases. But there was something about the Baker children she couldn't name or define.

So, Kealey found herself heading into the kennel area, learning from Wayne that the kids should be there. Just the kids, she told herself. Not Luke, just the kids. That's who she wanted to see.

Hearing voices, she paused. Brian's sounded agitated and immediately she was on alert.

"I'm sorry, Luke. I meant to have the kennels all cleaned up, but then practice took longer and I couldn't get here on time. But I won't do it again. I'll do better, I'll—"

Kealey charged toward the corner, prepared to confront Luke and to protect Brian.

But the big, incredibly masculine man had knelt down, his hands on Brian's shoulders. "I've told you this before. I meant it then and I mean it now." Luke paused, his voice husky with restrained emotion. "Maybe even more now. Chores or no chores, you have a place with me here. That's not going to change if a few kennels don't get cleaned on time. You understand?"

Brian's eyes filled with tears. "But I told you, too. I don't want to let you down."

"That's not going to happen. Brian, we all make mistakes. That's just part of life. The important thing is that you care about making things right, it's part of why you're going to grow up to be a good man." Luke's arms wrapped around the boy. "You believe me, don't you?"

When Brian finally pulled back, he brushed at his

eyes, nodding. "I wish you could be my father forever."

Frozen, Kealey watched as Luke's Adam's apple worked. "I wish I could be, too. But I want you to know even if that doesn't happen, you'll always have a place in my heart. Not just today, tomorrow, next week or even next year. I mean always."

Kealey fought the tears that were blurring her vision. As sure as she'd been that the children should be placed in a two-parent home, she knew now she was wrong. These three were exactly where they belonged, with the man who should raise them. She had been seeing the signs all along, even as she'd tried to ignore them. But there was no doubt, no possible opposing reasoning she could offer. The Baker children were crazy about Luke, and his feelings were clearly mutual.

A determination as fierce as the one she'd just witnessed gripped her. No matter what it took, she intended to make certain Luke and the Baker children stayed together.

Footsteps clattered loudly on the wooden stairs behind her. Troy and Hannah spotted her as they neared the bottom landing, their voices rising in pleased excitement. "Kealey!"

She walked rapidly toward them, raising her own voice. "Hi, guys! I was hoping to find you!"

"We like it when you're here," Troy told her.

Already emotional, Kealey had to firm her voice,

to keep from sounding too affected. "Now, that's the nicest thing anyone's said to me all day."

Troy's smile broadened.

It took so little to please these kids. And they had so very much to give.

"I was hoping maybe I could find someone to have ice cream with," Kealey told both Troy and Hannah, hoping the treat would lift Brian's spirits.

Grins erupted. "We could do that!" Hannah exclaimed.

"Uh-huh," Troy chimed in.

"You could?" Kealey asked, pretending to consider their offer. "And Brian, too?"

"Oh, but we have chores," Troy remembered suddenly.

Luke, accompanied by Brian, had just turned the corner toward the stairwell. Hearing the last of their conversation, Luke glanced at Troy and Hannah. "I think we could suspend them this once."

Kealey noticed that Brian lingered very close to Luke. And she realized in that instant that he needed to do the chores, to prove to Luke and perhaps himself that he could do the right thing.

"You know. If I helped, we could finish the chores sooner," Kealey offered. "Then, if Luke agrees, we could go for ice cream. Hey, even hamburgers. My treat." She met Luke's gaze, her own pleading for him to understand.

To her relief, he grasped her meaning instantly. "Hey, that's quite an offer, huh, guys? Tell you what, Kealey. I need Brian to do some of the more complicated duties. Would you mind helping Troy and Hannah instead?''

Kealey could have kissed him. ''That's great. I like petting the cats.''

''We have to sweep, too,'' Troy told her seriously.

''With a big strong boy like you to help, we'll have that done in no time,'' she replied, meeting Luke's gaze. She wasn't certain which direction the gratitude was flowing, but the feelings it was evoking were putting cracks in the dam she'd erected over a lifetime.

''I LIKE cheese on mine,'' Hannah told Luke over an hour later as they stood in line to order their hamburgers.

''You don't say,'' he responded in mock surprise.

She giggled. ''You knew that.''

The other two children gave their orders, then Kealey and Luke added theirs. The cashier tallied the total and Kealey withdrew her wallet.

''Hold on,'' Luke protested.

''My treat,'' she reminded him.

''I know social workers aren't exactly loaded.''

But instead of tensing up as he'd expected, a teasing grin sprouted on her lips. ''As opposed to veterinarians who take in every stray in the county?''

''Point taken. But I'm an old-fashioned guy.''

A bit of wonder and confusion colored her expression.

It occurred to him that he'd said that as though they were on a date. Even so he managed to put his money down on the counter first.

"Then I insist on paying for the ice cream cones," she retorted, rather than tussle for the bill.

He raised one brow in challenge. "You think so?"

Again, to his surprise, she reacted by curving her lips in reply. "We'll see."

Was it his imagination, or had she begun to loosen up—to not go rigid over the least little thing?

Once they were seated, Luke patiently helped Hannah with her hamburger, then poured ketchup for Troy's French fries. Glancing up, he caught Kealey's gaze on him, and he wondered what was going on behind those changing eyes of hers.

But Kealey didn't dare reveal her thoughts. How could she tell this incredible man that she was prepared to do whatever it took to make sure he and the children remained together? It went against her preconceived notions, but it was time to admit she was wrong. She didn't care what she might have to sacrifice, but if reversing her stand cost her this job, so be it. She'd moved around so much she'd become accustomed to starting over.

Brian was unusually quiet and Luke draped a casual, but bolstering arm over his shoulders. "You did a great job with the older dogs, today."

He nodded, not yet smiling. "I wish they had real

homes of their own. But they're so old nobody would want them.''

Kealey cleared her throat, her gaze darting from Brian to Luke. ''I was thinking about them the day we had the adoption party. It seems like people and pets kind of have to be matched up—so they're a good fit. Young families choose young animals— not necessarily puppies and kittens, but still young adult pets. They probably think an older dog or cat wouldn't have enough energy to play with their kids.''

''Probably,'' Luke agreed.

''Well, I was wondering if we could match up your older strays with older people, perhaps retired seniors who would like the companionship and appreciate the qualities of an older dog over a rambunctious puppy.''

Luke stared at her in amazement. He'd never even considered that possibility. It was more than that, though. She put so much thought, so much *original* thought into everything.

''Cool!'' Brian said, brightening for the first time. ''Do you really think we could do that?''

''It would take some research and work, but I think we could. I can contact Aging Services to see if they have a list of people living alone who might be good candidates.''

''And they could be 'dopted, too?'' Troy asked.

''In forever homes?'' Hannah echoed. ''Like us with Luke?''

Kealey's gaze didn't look so much startled as it did reflective, determined. "Sort of."

Luke again wondered at the change in her. And the change he felt when she was with them—with him.

CHAPTER NINE

KEALEY STARED at her supervisor, Jack Olson, in shocked dismay. "I know I requested a two-parent home for the Baker children, but the situation has changed. I'm in the process of preparing new documents."

Jack frowned. "Has he married?"

"No, but on further evaluation, it's become clear to me that he's providing a stable environment."

Shrugging, Jack started to turn away. "The Hendricks are fine foster parents and since the children in their care have been adopted, they have an opening."

"But—"

"Kealey, you know as well as I do that it's impossible to wait for a home that would accept all three children. I don't like dividing siblings any more than you do, but that's the harsh reality. At least two of them will be together and I have several new openings that can take the third child."

"Split them up?" Kealey whispered, more horrified than she'd imagined she could be.

"Kealey, you're not new to this. You know it happens all the time."

"Jack, why can't we leave them in Luke Duncan's care? The children are happy, becoming well adjusted—"

"You filed the papers with the court, remember?"

"I could talk to the judge," Kealey argued.

"That you could, but you wrote up a pretty persuasive argument on why they *shouldn't* be allowed to stay in a one-parent home. How do you plan to backtrack?"

Desperately, Kealey wondered that herself. She could envision the shattered expressions if she had to tell the children they would be split up, the agony she would cause them as well as Luke.

Everyone would be devastated, because she had been so sure she'd known best. So sure she'd refused to see the love between Luke Duncan and the Baker children until it was too late.

So sure she'd convinced a judge to trust her judgment.

And now Kealey wasn't nearly as sure she could fix what she had set in motion. If she couldn't, Luke would be right. As he'd predicted, to prove a point, she would be harming the children, yanking them from the one place they belonged. Remembering her newfound determination, she vowed *not* to let that happen.

SEVEN HOURS LATER Kealey knew she had lost. She'd tried every justification, every plea, every reasonable and unreasonable argument she could muster. She'd even requested an appeal from the state's attorney. But it was hard to win an argument when you suddenly switched sides.

The judge was kind but adamant. Having considered her original petition, he believed she was right to insist on placing the children with two-parent families. True, it was unfortunate that they would be split up, but a permanent resolution was the most prominent consideration. Realistically, he pointed out, few families would adopt all the Baker children.

As the hearing came to a close, Judge Allred pulled off his reading glasses. "Perhaps, Miss Fitzpatrick, we can hope that the right two-parent family will come along and adopt all three children."

And he refused to rescind the order, instead amending it to remove the children immediately.

Feeling horrible, ashamed and incredibly cruel for initiating this, Kealey finally accepted the judge's decision.

At the same time she knew she had to do *something,* anything to keep Luke and the children together. Perhaps her supervisor could help. Jack Olson carried a great deal of influence in the family court. But would it be enough?

As she rushed back to the office, a portion of the judge's last words continued to echo through her fractured thoughts. *Perhaps, Miss Fitzpatrick, the right two-parent family will adopt all three children.*

The *right* two-person family. The phrase re-sounded relentlessly, an unorthodox idea building.

The words continued to mock her even as she spent the last hours of the day and those of early evening behind closed doors with her supervisor, pleading Luke's case until she was convinced there was nothing Jack Olson could do, either. At least not yet.

If only she hadn't been so sure she was right. Just because her own experiences in single-parent homes had been negative she shouldn't have been so un-willing to believe there were exceptions.

Now, alone in her car as she drove toward Luke's house, she acknowledged for the first time that she'd allowed her own memories to cloud her judgment. By insisting on doing things her way, she had ruined all that—her actions alone were breaking up this family. And in the approaching darkness, she ac-knowledged a second, searing truth. Had another caseworker, *any* other caseworker been assigned, this wouldn't have happened. A different social worker would have seen beyond the limitations of a single father home to the benefits of a man who had grown to love these children as his own.

She swallowed against the choking truth. What she'd done was unforgivable—unless she remedied it. Luke would think she was crazy, perhaps she was, but she had to do something…she had to do the *right* thing. Late, true, but hopefully not too late.

Like it or not, she was the only one who could repair the damage.

Trying not to tremble, Kealey gathered her courage and pressed the doorbell. In a few moments a smiling Luke opened the door. Studying her face, his grin faded.

"What is it?"

"Where are the kids?" she asked, trying with all her might not to burst out the truth.

"Upstairs doing their homework."

"Can we talk?" she asked. "Privately?"

Again he searched her gaze. "Let's go into the backyard."

Once outside, they sat on the steps of the gazebo.

Luke spoke first. "It's bad, isn't it?"

Kealey twisted her hands together. "They found two-parent homes for the children."

"Homes? As in plural?"

She swallowed. "There wasn't enough space in one for all three kids. And we haven't turned up a solitary relative. From interviews with the kids, it's apparent there wasn't any extended family."

Luke's voice was grim, disappointed. "And you think it's best to split them up rather than have them live with me?"

Distress filled her voice. "Of course not! They love you and I think you love them."

He stared into the darkness.

"Do you?" she persisted.

"Yep. But I don't suppose that's going to do me any good, is it?"

Again she twisted her hands. "I honestly don't know. I went to court today. I argued on your behalf."

His eyes narrowed. "You did?"

"I realize that no one else can do a better job parenting them than you can. They're blossoming under your care. Separating the four of you would be heartbreaking…unforgivable."

A glimmer of hope crept over his expression. "Then why are you so glum? If I can keep—"

"That's just it. You can't."

"I don't get it, Kealey. You're the caseworker. If you recommend—"

"Before I knew… If you remember before—when I thought I knew what was right for you and them—I filed papers with the court, recommending they be relocated to a two-parent home."

"But surely you can tell them you've changed your mind."

"I did," she replied grimly.

"And?"

"The judge concurs with my first recommendation, especially in light of the fact that the kids would most likely be adopted once in a permanent home."

"What if I want to adopt them?"

She shrugged. "The judge's order supersedes

your request. He's insisting that the kids be removed tomorrow.''

"Tomorrow?'' he echoed in horrified shock.

"Yes. And your adoption request could be a problem. Even though they're more common these days, single parents still have a long, difficult task in adopting. As of tomorrow the kids will be in other foster homes. By the time your request could be processed they might already be adopted by someone else.''

"So that's it?'' Luke asked dully. "Even though I'm sure I want to adopt them?''

"Maybe not.'' She hesitated, remembering the heated, unusual conversation, Jack Olson's disbelief. "My supervisor and I believe the judge would allow you to keep the children if you *were* a two-parent family.''

Confused, he stared at her. "What am I supposed to do? Get married?''

Kealey took a deep breath, feeling the pressure of her nerves pushing at her lungs, threatening to choke her. "Yes. I think that would do it.''

"And I'm supposed to produce a wife in— what?—twenty-four, forty-eight hours?''

She nodded, her eyes huge and luminescent in the moonlight.

"Where am I…'' His words trailed off, his gaze locking with hers. "Kealey?'' he asked in baffled wonder.

Again she nodded as she tried to restrain her

nerves, knowing that she had no alternative to offer, also knowing she alone needed to take responsibility, to provide a solution. Unless he had another prospective bride in mind, she was his only hope to keep his new family together. "For the children."

"The children," he repeated, his gaze darkening, questioning.

Kealey had attempted to rapidly formulate a plan in the few hours she'd had to consider this desperate strategy. She knew it would sound insane. "I thought we could make an arrangement upfront that protects us both. We can set a time limit—I'm thinking until the judge grants you permanent custody, which may take a while. If you want to set a definite time period, that's all right, too. Of course, we'll have to tell the children the truth— I wouldn't want to disappoint them with an unrealistic fantasy." Kealey paused, desperately wondering what he was thinking. "I suppose it would be best to tell your family the truth, as well. I wouldn't want to hurt them, either."

"I think they'll take it all right. My parents learned a long time ago that I have to do things in my own way. But what about your family? What will they think of this?"

Her laugh wasn't brittle, though she felt as if she were about to break. "There isn't any family to consult. I grew up in foster homes."

"Which is why you care so much about the kids."

Her chin dropped a fraction. It was so incredibly difficult to reveal herself. She'd never been able to quash the fear of allowing anyone to get too close. "Yes. My mother abandoned me when I was five and I never knew my father."

He made a sympathetic noise, but she waved it away. "I don't need your pity, Luke, but you deserve to know the truth."

His eyes were warm, yet he injected a light note in his voice. "So you're trying to tell me your side of the guest list will be small?"

Kealey felt an unexpected moment of relief. "Yes, I guess so."

"Maybe it's something we can discuss more when we're old married folks."

She stiffened. "It's only a *temporary* arrangement."

He met her eyes. "Accepted."

The air between them was weighty, heavy with emotions that couldn't be spoken aloud.

Nervously, she nibbled her dry lips, realizing how unlike her it was to act on impulse—especially one this wild, so unexpected. "I suppose you think I'm awfully brazen."

"Brazen? Hmmm." He shook his head as his gaze roamed over her again. "Nope, not the word I'm thinking."

"Luke, I know my first assessment was wrong, but despite what you might think, it wasn't personal, not toward you, I mean. Although I now realize I shouldn't have been so obstinate, I truly only wanted what was best for the kids. They deserve the finest and—''

Gently he laid two fingers over her lips. ''I know. I mouthed off a lot when I first met you, or should I say when I met you for the second time. Rachel's right. You do care. But are you sure about this? It seems the children and I have everything to gain, but you...''

Kealey had never been less sure of anything in her life. But she couldn't allow her own shortsighted decision to ruin four lives. ''I caused the situation. It's my responsibility to find a solution. But I guess the better question would be, are you sure?''

His eyes darkened to near black and Kealey wished desperately she could see what he hid behind the dark shield. ''You know I want to keep the kids, Kealey, and I'll do whatever it takes.''

It wasn't exactly the golden proposal most women dreamed of, but this wasn't a real marriage. Still, she wished the prospect of her as a wife hadn't been uttered as though he'd volunteered to take a dose of cod liver oil. Swallowing, she gave him the last of the news.

''I spoke to my supervisor and he thinks the judge will go along with our request, but nothing in the legal system's a certainty until every *i* is dotted. We'll have to file an emergency motion first thing in the morning.''

''But you're game to try?''

Kealey nodded, knowing she couldn't go back on her promise, also knowing she'd never been so frightened in her life.

THE JUDGE was dubious. But he had worked with Jack Olson for many years and respected his opinion. Without his recommendation, Judge Allred would have been tempted to stick to his original order to immediately remove the children from the Duncan home.

At the barest minimum it was unorthodox. A social worker marrying a foster parent to create a home for three orphans. But it wasn't the oddest thing he'd ever seen. After all, this was the U.S. justice system.

The judge stared down his long, thin nose. Kealey knew from past experience that despite his forbidding demeanor, he had only the best interest of the children in mind. He hadn't chosen a career in family law for fame and fortune.

"Mr. Duncan, I see that you've also filed a petition for adoption. While that's admirable, you do realize that the children's interest is the court's foremost concern?"

Luke stood tall, self-assured, certain. "Yes, Your Honor."

"You also realize that I will order strict monitoring from Child Services regarding this case. Any irregularities and the previous order will be reinstated."

"Yes, Your Honor."

"And, Miss Fitzpatrick, I understand from your superiors that you have an impeccable record. You're putting your professional career on the line as well as your personal one. I assume Mr. Olson has already informed you that if this turns into a debacle your career will head south."

Kealey swallowed. "Yes, Your Honor."

Judge Allred studied both Kealey and Luke. Finally, he pushed back his glasses, then scrawled a signature on the new court order. "This goes against my better judgment, but I'm granting you temporary custody of the three minor Baker children, Brian, Hannah and Troy. I will, of course, expect proof of your marriage in seven days' time."

Luke and Kealey nodded in unison.

"I truly hope you've both thought this decision through, examined all the consequences, and most importantly, that you're thinking of the children, rather than yourselves." He glanced over at his court officer. "Schedule a follow-up hearing in sixty days, Ms. Williams."

The court officer made the notation.

"Then we're done here," the judge announced.

"Thank you, Your Honor," Luke replied. "For giving us this chance. We won't disappoint you."

Judge Allred looked reflective and not completely convinced. "I hope not."

A few minutes later, walking away from the

courtroom, Luke found he was still holding his breath. Slowly releasing it, he realized Kealey hadn't said anything since they'd left the judge's presence. And he was pretty certain she wasn't daydreaming about an elaborate white wedding. She'd made crystal clear that her intentions were to keep this marriage solely a practical arrangement.

"Kealey?"

She glanced up at him, her eyes unguarded. "I was so afraid we wouldn't win."

It wasn't the answer he'd expected. "You were?"

She nodded. "If my supervisor hadn't helped…"

"But he did," Luke responded gently. "Sometimes that's all we have in this life, Kealey. Help from friends, family, even supervisors."

Her smile was watery, and so untypically Kealey. "Sounds like a Duncan family pep talk coming on."

"Ooh." He hunched his shoulders in mock horror. "Didn't realize we had the act down so pat."

This time her smile was fuller. "You've been working on it for a long time."

"Yeah, well you'd better start rehearsing yourself."

She blinked in question.

"Don't forget. You'll be a Duncan soon as well."

Kealey couldn't have looked more surprised if he'd suddenly sprouted wings.

"Hadn't considered that aspect?"

"Well…" She tried to clear her throat, failed,

then swallowed again. "We haven't had a lot of time for thinking."

"Something the judge obviously clued in on." Luke couldn't forget the man's face, his obvious doubt. But then he'd had a mass of doubts himself. Not the least of which had been his shock at Kealey's suggestion.

While Luke didn't doubt that he'd grown to love the children, he could scarcely believe Kealey would uproot her entire life for them. Nor could he believe how his own feelings for her were changing by the day, how it had occurred to him but not her that their relationship could be more than temporary.

Only one doubt remained. Kealey had made her offer based on her affection for the children, her guilt over causing the situation, the belief that he would be a good father. But she'd never mentioned her feelings for him.

The afternoon was dwindling toward dusk, a time of questions and doubt. A time when nothing seemed clear. Kealey was walking only a few inches away from him, close enough for him to take her into his arms, to test out her feelings. Then she turned, a fragile, exposed look eclipsing her normal confidence.

Instinct kicking in, Luke reached for her hand. She stiffened only nominally. And although she relaxed a fraction, Luke realized they were far from where they needed to be. He just hoped it wasn't impossibly far.

RACHEL STUDIED Kealey critically in the pink-lit dressing room. "You're not really thinking of wearing *that!*"

Kealey smoothed the slim skirt of the tailored suit. "What's wrong with it?"

Rachel sputtered and rolled her eyes in a simultaneous motion. "Do you really have to ask?"

"It's practical—"

"Practical's for work, even church, possibly shopping, but *not* for your wedding!"

"It's not like this is a real wedding," Kealey demurred.

"You don't know my brother," Rachel muttered.

Kealey's head whipped up with amazing speed. "What did you say?"

"Just thinking out loud about my maid of honor duties." Rachel's expression narrowed. "You *are* going to ask me, aren't you?"

Stupefied, Kealey realized she'd never thought of a maid of honor. She'd never believed she would ever get married, and she'd certainly never before had any close friends in whom she could confide dreams of weddings. "It's going to be casual. Is it appropriate to have attendants?"

Rachel shrugged. "You're the bride. Ergo you decide what's appropriate." She managed to look forlorn. "Of course if you don't *want* me to be your maid of honor…"

Guilt had stabbed more steadily in the past forty-eight hours than it had in a lifetime. "It's not that—"

"Then what?" Rachel asked, her expression a trifle too innocent.

"Rachel Duncan, you're wasted in child services. I hear SWAT teams are always looking for negotiators. Fine. You think I need a maid of honor, so I'll have one."

"With a gracious request like that, how could I refuse?" Rachel studied the suit Kealey was wearing. "But if I'm in this wedding, we're definitely not doing dowdy."

"We're not?" Kealey asked weakly, a small part of her wanting something less practical, something more romantic, certainly more alluring.

"You've got Luke. I still have to think of my future prospects." Rachel's brows rose speculatively. "And he could be on the guest list."

It was Kealey's turn to sputter. "I don't *have* Luke. This isn't that kind of marriage."

"Hmm."

"Rachel!"

"You know, with your skin I don't think pure white is flattering."

Slightly distracted, Kealey glanced into the mirror. "It's not?"

"You were blessed with that peaches-and-cream skin. Why not let it glow?" Rachel shook her head. "Face it. We're in the wrong store, chum."

"We are?"

"I thought so when I walked in," Rachel replied. She studied the suit again. "Now I'm sure."

Kealey found a bit of her usual resistance returning. "I'm not wearing a traditional wedding gown. I told you that."

"And I'm not arguing. But you don't have to dress like your grandmother, either. Come on. I know just the store."

Kealey glanced into the mirror one more time. "Well, I guess you could be right."

"Good thing we have all day," Rachel mused.

Kealey unzipped the skirt. "Oh?"

But Rachel's expression only grew more enigmatic.

"I'll meet you out front. Bells on your toes!"

TWO HOURS LATER, Kealey looked at her friend in exasperation. "Bells in your belfry's more like it. You didn't tell me the perfect dress in the perfect store was in Houston."

"Did you really think our little Greenville could produce the dream dress?"

"I don't recall asking for the *dream* dress!"

"More's the pity," Rachel replied blithely. "And stop complaining." She turned off the busy intersection onto a slightly quieter side street. "We're here."

"We aren't planning to hop the Concorde for Paris just in case this shop doesn't have *the* dress, are we?"

Rachel's face was smug. "No need. Trust me. It will be here."

They stepped into the shop, La Boutique de Mariage. At first all Kealey could think of was wringing her friend's neck. Chic, but traditional wedding gowns lined the walls. True, they were beautiful gowns, but she wasn't going to be pushed into one.

Rachel hooked their arms together. "Wipe that look of horror off your face or Miss Lily will think you're having a heart attack."

"I just might be. Rachel, I told you—"

"Have faith, Kealey." Her voice had gentled.

Since they'd already driven for hours, Kealey reluctantly nodded. And taking another glance around the shop, she had to admit it was an incredible place, almost magical in atmosphere. It seemed to contain everything a perfect wedding required. And that was the thought that sobered Kealey. Hers was not to be a perfect wedding, rather a pretend one.

Just then a tiny woman emerged from the rear of the store. Expecting a tall, ravishing French woman dripping with disdain, she was shocked to see this grandmotherly figure. But then perhaps she was the seamstress.

Rachel held out her arms. "Miss Lily."

The elderly woman's face transformed in welcome and Kealey could see that once she had been quite pretty. "Rachel, I'd begun to despair about your wedding gown," she replied in a soft voice tinged with only the barest trace of an accent.

Rachel smiled gently. "All in good time. I'm not

here for me today. This is my friend and future sister-in-law, Kealey Fitzpatrick.''

Lily took Kealey's hand, looking deeply in her eyes. ''And for this one, something as exquisite as she is, and almost as important, something nontraditional.''

Kealey gasped, touched by the compliment, amazed by the woman's insight. ''How did you know that?''

''It's what I do,'' Lily responded simply. ''For all of my life. You want a miracle. And you want it soon.''

Kealey swallowed, then glanced at Rachel.

But Rachel's smile was knowing, rather than smug. ''No, I didn't call ahead. Miss Lily is a wonder. And that's why she's the preeminent wedding designer and consultant in the state.''

For a moment Kealey wavered, thinking of her not overly generous salary. ''I would like something special, but I do have a budget…''

Miss Lily waved her hands. ''Let us talk of dresses and tiaras and satin slippers.''

Helplessly, Kealey followed as Miss Lily turned and headed toward the rear of the store.

Once in the inner room, she caught her breath. It seemed they were awash in silk, satin and chiffon. But it wasn't the ordinary, not even the typical. These dresses were softer, unique.

Even Rachel drew in her breath. ''Oh, my.''

Miss Lily walked straight to one dress, and lifted

it from the rack. But rather than holding it up for Kealey to view, she motioned for her to step into the dressing room.

Kealey considered asking to see the rest of the selection, but there was something in Miss Lily's eyes that quashed the request.

A few minutes later she stepped out of the room and up onto the pedestal area that was flanked on all sides by mirrors.

"Oh, Kealey," Rachel murmured.

It was just a slip of a dress, a creamy ivory strapless frock. Kealey hesitantly touched the delicate lace that seemed to shimmer over the silk.

"It's Irish lace," Lily explained. "Seemed appropriate."

Although she'd never known her roots, Kealey was aware that with a name like Fitzpatrick her ancestors must have come from somewhere in Ireland. But people without families rarely considered heritage.

Miss Lily met her gaze. "It suits you."

Haltingly, Kealey lifted her head, staring into the mirror. It was a dream of a dress, not the traditional full-skirted wedding gown, yet something incredibly special.

"It's perfect. And you look perfect in it."

Kealey resisted the urge to blush. Still her gaze slid sideways to view her friend. "You really like it?"

But Rachel didn't joke. Instead her eyes misted. "It was made for you."

Kealey thought of her budget and for once in her adult life practicality flew out the window. "Then I guess we'll have to buy it."

Rachel's smile shone through her tears. "Yes! And Mom will be so pleased!"

"Your mother?"

"Oh, didn't I tell you? This is where she bought her wedding gown, as did Mary and Ruth. It's sort of a family tradition."

Kealey clamped down on her bottom lip so hard it almost started the tears she was trying to halt. Family tradition. She, Kealey Fitzpatrick, part of a family. Miss Lily was right. They *had* come to this store seeking a miracle.

CHAPTER TEN

SUNSHINE SWEETENED the blooming roses, age old bushes that rambled around the borders of the spacious yard. The faded Victorian house, the fluttering paper lanterns, the towering magnolia tree—all looked as though they'd been plucked from a previous century, a calmer, slower time. A collection of wicker chairs and tables gathered by the Duncan family completed the illusion.

Actually, it was the Duncans themselves who completed the illusion. Dressed in their Sunday finery, Luke's parents, all his siblings, their spouses, and many children filled the grounds. The youngest girls wore long, flowing chiffon dresses, making up an entire squadron of flower girls. Even though they'd been clued in as to the purpose and probable duration of the marriage, the family had insisted on helping to make the day perfect.

A weathered white trellis was decorated by nature's hand, honeysuckle and bougainvillea trailing effortlessly over and around the old wood. Beneath it, buffet tables, covered in linen tablecloths procured by Ruth, were filled with food also provided by the Duncans. Even the towering wedding cake had an old-fashioned aura. Fresh flowers decorated each layer and the sugary marzipan frosting had been colored to match Kealey's dress.

And for a moment Kealey wanted to pinch herself. Surely it couldn't be real, this beautiful, perfect setting, this seemingly wonderful family. Again she touched the single strand of pearls at her neck, family pearls Jane had loaned her. They were Jane's own wedding pearls, the ones her mother had worn, the ones her own daughters had worn. Kealey had tried to refuse, but she couldn't squelch the pleasure in Jane's eyes, nor could she completely suppress her own desire to wear something so traditional, to pretend even for a day that she truly was part of the family. Jane had told her that this day would be special, regardless of the outcome of their union, one she maintained should be as memorable as the bride and groom themselves.

Peeking around the corner of the gate, Kealey glimpsed Luke. Vaguely she wondered if she was remembering to breathe. He'd always looked handsome, but today...

She'd never seen him dressed in anything but casual clothes. Now he looked as though he could have stepped from the pages of *GQ*. The European cut of his suit accentuated his tall, lean form, just as the crisp white of his shirt showed off his tan.

His father clapped Luke on his back, then turned toward Kealey, winking as he walked toward her.

Reaching her side, his smile broadened. "Luke's

liable to faint dead away when he sees you. You look mighty pretty, Kealey.''

Again, an unfamiliar blush threatened. She had been so touched when Timothy had offered to give her away. Luke's oldest brother, Peter, was his best man. However, Luke had asked Brian and Troy to stand up with him as well.

Luke and Kealey had talked with the children extensively, explaining that the arrangement was to be short-term, that it was something they were doing so that Luke could keep them permanently. Hannah had anxiously asked if they could treat Kealey like a parent as well. Unable to refuse this request, they had said yes, also agreeing that for the duration of their time together, they would behave as any typical family. The children had also been told that the wedding was the first day of Luke and Kealey's ''marriage'' and that their adoption by Luke would mark the last day.

Despite this sobering news, young Hannah shone as Kealey's junior bridesmaid. And Rachel's deep fuchsia dress was the perfect foil to Hannah's girlish frilly pink frock.

One by one, Rachel and Hannah started down the bridal path.

Kealey swallowed, glancing up at Luke's father for reassurance.

He squeezed her arm. ''Now if I get light-headed, you prop me up, okay?''

For a moment she stared at him in alarm, but then

she saw the teasing glint in his eye. Taking a deep breath, she smiled at him in gratitude. Then, clutching her bouquet, they started across the lawn.

The minister stood on the top step of the gazebo. On the right, Luke stood tall, his face sober as he watched her approach. Although Peter, Brian and Troy stood beside him, Kealey could only see Luke.

Luke was equally focused. Amazingly, despite the crowd of family and friends, it seemed that Kealey was the only person he could see. Mouth dry, he could only stare.

Her dress looked like some magical thing. In no way traditional, the flowing silk and lace swirled around her as though with a life of its own. Kealey's long golden hair was partially swept up, a few soft tendrils curling about her face, some cascading over the long, loose waves that flowed over her shoulders. Among the strands was a delicate pearl tiara.

As he watched, she removed one hand from her bouquet of ivory and pink roses. Discreetly she stroked one of the pearl teardrop earrings he had given her. Although she'd averted her face when he'd presented her with the gift, he was sure that he'd glimpsed the beginnings of a few tears.

She'd tried to return the earrings, and he'd half expected her to refuse to wear them today. But they graced her delicate lobes, sunlight glinting on the ivory pearls.

She was a vision, soft, romantic, enticing, incredible. It took his entire concentration to remain standing in place when all he wanted was to pull her into his arms to see if she could possibly be real.

Then she was standing beside him. The pastor uttered a few words and his father moved aside. Then it was time to take her hand. To his amazement, it trembled within his. A fierce protectiveness rose in unison with his desire. Could this be the same cold, rigid woman who'd sent him running on their blind date?

The pastor continued to speak. Words as old as love and marriage itself.

Luke was a traditional guy, a man who'd always assumed he would meet and marry the love of his life and in time have children with her. That together they would form a family much like the one he'd been raised in, then grow old together.

Now, however, he was standing beside a woman he'd scarcely begun to know. True, he was wildly attracted to her. But deep in his consciousness, he had begun to acknowledge that his feelings for her were strong, increasingly strong.

Kealey, however, hadn't reciprocated those feelings, had never spoken of anything other than a businesslike arrangement for their marriage. Was that enough for him?

Then he looked at the Baker children, their eyes shining in hope and excitement. Luke's grip on Kealey's hand tightened. He would make it enough.

Studying Kealey, Luke watched her eyes close briefly when the words *till death do you part* were uttered. But her eyes widened when it was time to exchange the rings. He knew from Rachel that Kealey had purchased a simple band for him. She probably thought he'd done the same. She clearly wasn't prepared for the exquisite antique gold band that he slipped on her finger.

She looked to him questioningly, but he kept his expression blank. It wouldn't do to tell her its origin.

Then in seeming moments, it was time to kiss his bride.

It was only a kiss. An innocent touching of lips, just a symbol.

But he made the mistake of looking into her eyes as his head angled ever so slightly. And those ever-changing eyes captured him, shining with a combination of fear and hope. He couldn't help himself then—he had to give her a real kiss.

Then applause broke out, drowning out the private moment, bringing them back to reality. Family and friends surrounded them, exchanging hugs and congratulations.

The children, having been given small bottles of soap, opened them and soon, huge iridescent bubbles filled the yard. Some of the bubbles were enormous, and when they burst, the children laughed in delight.

Jane and Timothy hugged both Luke and Kealey long and hard, each trying unsuccessfully to disguise the tears in their eyes.

Watching them, Kealey felt her own eyes

moisten. Surely, she hadn't felt this tearful since she'd been an abandoned child. And then for such very different reasons.

But it's not real! she screamed inwardly. As perfect and beautiful as it all was, none of it was real.

Then Luke's hand was on her elbow as music, provided by a talented quartet of his nieces and nephews, filled the air.

"I believe this dance is mine," he told her quietly.

Even more uncertain, Kealey nodded, turning to fit into his arms. Why did it seem so right to be there, she wondered desperately, knowing how temporary their marriage would be.

As the guests stepped back, creating a space for them, Luke led them in an old-fashioned waltz. And somewhere in the gentle swirling motions of the dance, amid the huge circle of his family and friends, she fell in love with him. She'd known all along that her feelings had been shifting out of control. But she hadn't known her heart could ignore her logic and become helplessly, hopelessly his.

The music tapered off and in the hush, Kealey met Luke's eyes. But they were dark and unreadable. Was he already regretting this?

Then their guests surrounded them again, their joyful voices filling the air, their laughter spilling through the romantic moment.

Tearing her gaze from her brand-new husband, Kealey looked for the children. While Hannah and

Troy looked elated, Brian furtively wiped a tear from his eyes. She walked over to him and knelt beside him. "Hey, how's my little man?"

Brian shrugged, still unable to voice his feelings. Knowing exactly how he felt, she gently kissed his forehead. "I think the tradition is that this dance is ours."

He scuffed his right shoe into the grass. "I don't know how to dance."

She leaned closer and whispered, "I'm not so good, either. Maybe we can make each other look better."

He lowered his eyes, then lifted them cautiously. "You sure?"

Her smile bloomed. "Absolutely."

Together they walked to the makeshift dance floor, the circle of grass designated for that purpose. Kealey kept her steps slow and easy. With great deliberation, his face scrunched into a mask of concentration, Brian followed her lead.

Glancing up, Kealey saw that Luke was dancing with Hannah, making her giggle with delight. Rachel reached for Troy's hand, coaxing him to dance as well.

When the dance was over, another round of applause broke out.

Jane Duncan's eyes were suspiciously moist as she approached Kealey. "That was the sweetest thing I've ever seen."

Still unsettled by all these open feelings, Kealey could only smile.

That, however, didn't seem to faze Jane. She took one of Kealey's hands. "I'm delighted to have another daughter."

At a complete loss for words, Kealey could only swallow against the rush of unwanted emotion. "You know—"

"I know what I know," Jane replied enigmatically. Then she glanced up, seeing her son approaching. "I'm sure your groom wants to claim you," she said before slipping away.

"You've completely won her over," Luke told Kealey, thinking again how beautiful she looked.

"Your mother's a special person," Kealey murmured.

But Luke didn't reply to her comment. Instead, he gently cupped one of the teardrop earrings. "I wasn't sure you'd wear them."

Her gaze turned touchingly shy. It was so uncharacteristic, it unsettled him even more. Especially when she didn't answer immediately.

"They're perfect with the pearls your mother lent me," she explained finally.

Vaguely disappointed, he wondered if that was the only reason. Not yet ready to believe that she hadn't done it simply to please herself—or even him—he took her hand. "One dance wasn't enough."

She nodded, and he wondered what she thought the timbre of her voice would have revealed.

Despite the noise of conversation, laughter and music he could discern the subtle swish of her dress, the gliding of silk against skin, the quiet rush of her breath, the nearly silent sigh as the music wound to an end.

They were again claimed by friends and relatives, yet Luke could still feel the warmth of her body pressed against his, the indention of her breasts against his chest, the alluring brush of her hips against his. How could it be that she was nearly the length of the yard away, yet the feeling was so real he expected her to still be in his arms?

Like all Duncan family functions, this one had no end in sight. Luke's mother, sisters and sisters-in-law discreetly kept the tables replenished while tidying at the same time. As the afternoon crawled toward twilight, there was no huge mess to clean. And Luke's brothers had already arranged to pick up the tables and extra furniture the following day.

Brian, Troy and Hannah were going home with their new foster grandparents. Jane and Timothy were insistent, convinced that, despite the circumstances, Luke and Kealey needed to be alone. And the kids were excited by the prospect of having grandparents for the first time in their lives. Their natural grandparents had passed away before Brian was born. Their mother had been an only child and their father's single brother had died in childhood.

Having never known the joys of an extended family, the kids thought the Duncans were fantastic.

Kealey and Luke waved goodbye as the last of their guests departed. Glancing at each other and then away, they entered the quiet house.

The all too quiet house.

Kealey fiddled with the lace on her dress, realizing despite the spaciousness of the house, that it seemed terribly intimate. Usually the old Victorian was filled with sounds of Brian, Troy and Hannah. Even when they were in school, Wayne was usually around in the clinic, but, he, too, had left after the wedding. Even the animals seemed unusually quiet and still.

"Maybe we should check on the cats and dogs," she suggested hopefully.

His gaze took a long walk over her as though appraising each inch. "Wayne already took care of that. Besides, I think we're just a tad overdressed for kennel duty."

"We could change—"

He grabbed her hand. "Not just yet."

Self-consciously, she glanced down at the amazing gown. "I'm not used to wearing dresses like this."

"It was a special occasion," he reminded her.

Kealey wished he would stop looking at her like that. It's just the dress, she wanted to tell him, nothing else about her had changed.

Nothing...

But her new feelings would make a liar out of her.

"I saved one bottle of champagne," Luke announced, walking to the sideboard that held an ice bucket. Before he reached for the champagne, however, he paused. Kealey heard the scrape of a match, smelled the pungent burst of sulphur, then watched as he lit two fat candles that flanked the ice bucket.

Mesmerized by the flickering light, she swallowed nervously. "We had a toast earlier."

"This one's just for us," he replied.

"Oh," she responded, wondering why her voice sounded so small. With great effort, she put more force into her next words. "Don't tell me you have an extra wedding cake tucked away as well."

"Nah, I think we did that okay the first time."

And they had.

Kealey remembered flinching, expecting he would follow the recent, boorish habit of smashing the cake into her face. Instead, he'd gently offered her a small bite, then reached out, wiping away a small bit of frosting that had edged her lips. Just thinking of that touch sent her stomach into a dive.

But Kealey recognized her own vulnerability, the likelihood that she had read far more into a simple touch than it warranted. Even if Luke did feel a physical connection, it would be only that.

Surprised that she still harbored even a fraction of that dream, she backed away. Immediately, an offended yowl greeted her.

Turning, she saw the cats, Kate and Spencer, just behind her. Uncertain which one she'd trod upon, she knelt down. "Sorry, guys."

"They're always underfoot." Luke crossed the room, carrying two full champagne flutes. "I'm so used to it, I forget they're there."

"I'm not even sure who I stepped on," Kealey confessed.

Luke looked between the cats, one black, the other white. "Okay, fess up, who got under Kealey's feet?"

In typical cat fashion, they ignored Luke, the black one scooting closer to Kealey. She reached out to pet the cat. "I hate to admit this, but I'm not sure who's who."

Luke smiled. "The white is Kate, the black Spencer."

"Unusual names," Kealey mused.

"Well, I'm a big fan of Hepburn and Tracy, so…"

Startled, yet feeling as though a piece of an unknown puzzle had just clicked in place, she stared at him. "You like their movies?"

"I'm a sucker for anything from that time period." He studied her closely. "How about you?"

Kealey considered confessing her love of Hepburn and Tracy, her amazement that they shared this unusual connection, but it wasn't in her to do so. "Yes," she replied, not realizing the tone of her voice had changed. "I like them a lot."

"I feel a video night coming on."

She smiled unexpectedly. "Brian, Troy and Hannah could become the only aficionados in elementary school."

"They're already known as the dog and cat kids," he told her, lifting his glass to gently clink the delicate flute against hers. "To you, Mrs. Duncan."

She froze; it wasn't in her to fake a response, to pretend his words hadn't shaken her.

"It's okay, Kealey. I know the boundaries of our agreement."

Boundaries. That sounded so cold, so technical. But that's what their arrangement was. Trying to maintain her composure, she nodded, then took a sip of champagne.

Her hand tightened around the fragile stem of the flute. "These are beautiful glasses."

His smile was unexpectedly pleased. "They're the family wedding flutes. They were a gift to my great-grandparents for their wedding and they've been used by all the Duncans since then."

All this family, this tradition. Incredibly touched, she was at the same time painfully aware how she didn't fit in.

Luke didn't press, instead glancing at the staircase. They had only briefly discussed the sleeping arrangements and it was still an awkward subject. Kealey had seen the kids' rooms when she'd made her in-home inspections and knew that Brian and Troy shared one room. Hannah had a smaller one.

The only other bedroom upstairs was Luke's. They had agreed there was no other choice but to share. The house's original floor plan had a small study and conservatory on the main floor, but they had been combined into the clinic space. And Luke had told her that he'd converted the fourth bedroom upstairs into a master bathroom. Although the attic could be renovated, there wasn't time to do so before their wedding. Besides, they'd reasoned, they were adults who could handle the situation.

But reason seemed far away at the moment.

Kealey cleared her throat. "I put my overnight bag upstairs, in…your room."

Unblinking, Luke nodded.

Silence thundered between them, and Kealey clenched the skirt of her gown, looking as though she might bolt.

Luke glanced at the nervous gesture. "I know what we discussed, but I can bunk on the couch."

Kealey ran an agitated hand over her forehead. "And how's that going to look to the kids? We told them that for the duration of our marriage, we'd be a real family. They've watched enough television to know that the dad's not supposed to sleep on the sofa. I didn't cancel the lease on my apartment just to make an appearance for the court. Kids are intuitive. If they see you sleeping on the couch, they'll think something's wrong. I don't want that."

"We *are* mature adults," Luke responded in what he hoped was a normal tone, since the thought itself was insane.

"And we should be able to share the same room," she added in a nervous tone. "It's not as though we're like average newlyweds."

But Luke couldn't answer. More than simple tension flowed between them. A new word would have to be invented to define the pressure that bent the air.

The house was still incredibly quiet. Then he looked at Kealey's hands. She was twisting them, her nerves and fragility evident. And, despite the desire to accept her offer, he had to do the right thing. "Tomorrow, when the kids are home, we'll tackle sharing the bedroom. But tonight I'll take the couch."

"You don't have to," she replied, unable to hide the relief in her voice. "I could—"

He held out his hand. "You could dance with me again." He glanced at the two candles that still flickered on the sideboard. "Until they've burned down."

Trepidation, anticipation, uncertainty, and possibly a trace of hope—all cascaded over her face in mere seconds. Luke knew he'd done the right thing.

He wondered if that righteous thought would keep him warm through the night. He suspected, instead, that he would spend it tossing and turning. And holding her in his arms in one slow dance after another was just going to make it much worse. But glancing down at her beautiful eyes, he decided it was worth the sacrifice.

CHAPTER ELEVEN

THE NEXT DAY was even more tense than Kealey had anticipated, despite many distractions. The children, returned by Luke's parents because the following day meant school, had been excited to share the details of their sleepover. It seemed the senior Duncans were a huge hit.

Shortly after they returned home, however, Hannah had a small crisis with Miss Tansy. The cat had wandered off and the child was certain she was gone for good. Knowing how fragile the children still were, they'd set out to search. Within a short time Luke had found the errant cat, a rush of joy ensued and the evening kept advancing.

Earlier in the day, Kealey had taken an inordinately long time to collect her clothing from her apartment and bring it back to the house. It seemed terribly intimate to hang her things in the closet next to Luke's.

The reality of what she'd committed to finally hit her. She still had some boxes to pack, but she'd never been one to collect things. The few possessions she'd ever been given as a child had been taken away or lost in her many moves. And as an adult she'd never come to truly believe anything was permanent. So, all she owned besides clothing were a very few toiletries and a lean supply of household goods, not even a complete set of china or cookware.

The furniture was rented along with the apartment. Her landlord had been both understanding and lenient in allowing her to cancel the lease once she told him the reason for the sudden move.

Everyone seemed to be understanding, thoughtful. But that didn't keep Kealey's nerves at bay. Had she been completely nuts to insist on maintaining the appearance of being truly married? That couch was looking better and better. Then she'd remember three earnest little faces, and her internal debate continued.

Even dinner seemed to zoom by in a flash.

Luke insisted on helping with the dishes.

"I really can do this on my own," she told him, desperately dreading any more time spent alone with him. He seemed too near, too attractive....

"No need to," he replied, placing a plate up in one of the higher cabinets. "I'm used to washing a lot of dishes. One of the pitfalls of a big family, too much cleaning up."

But Kealey couldn't smile at his lighthearted attempt at conversation.

His voice remained casual, easy. "I rented a few movies."

Relieved, she washed the last plate. Movies had

always been an escape for her. And if it meant delaying the moment when they had to go upstairs, she wouldn't even mind watching a macho action film or a Disney tale.

She lifted her hands from the soapy water and reached for the sprayer.

Luke intercepted her hands, then lifted the spray nozzle to gently rinse the suds away. It was a little thing, probably something he'd done without particular thought. Yet, she stared at their joined hands, amazed that such a domestic chore could seem so much more.

He picked up the dish towel, carefully drying her hands, the basic cotton as sensual as the most exotic silk.

Kealey wasn't certain if her breath slowed, quickened…or perhaps stopped altogether.

They might have stood that way all night, overcome by some sort of temporary paralysis, but Troy burst into the kitchen.

"I can help with the popcorn so we can see the movies," Troy offered cheerfully.

Luke didn't reply at first. And it took several more moments before he grudgingly released Kealey's hands to turn to Troy. His voice when he spoke, was uncommonly husky. "That's movie for you. Just one, not plural. And yes, you can help us with the popcorn."

"But you got a *bunch* of videos!" Troy protested.

"So I did. But grown-ups get to stay up later than children."

Kealey's gaze flew to his. However, she didn't see any hidden meaning to the words.

In short time, they popped the popcorn, collected bowls and trooped into the living room. Luke inserted a video, while the children sprawled on the floor. Then he settled beside Kealey on the couch.

Although the kids were open to watching any kind of movie, they looked baffled when the black-and-white credits began to roll.

Kealey turned to stare at Luke. "*Pat and Mike?* You rented a Hepburn and Tracy movie?"

He nodded.

Although she wanted to beam with pleasure, she eyed the children with dismay as she lowered her voice. "They aren't going to like it."

He shrugged. "It'll expand their horizons."

"Possibly. But it might also put them to sleep." Yet Kealey was incredibly touched that Luke had chosen these particular videos. He'd obviously read more into her casual comment that she, too, liked the Hepburn-Tracy movies than she'd realized. Was she becoming more transparent? Or was Luke growing to know and see more of her than she'd realized?

The prospect was unsettling, yet somehow it crept beneath her skin and went straight to her heart. Falling into the black-and-white world of cinema that she loved, Kealey found her nerves calming bit by bit, scene by scene.

"Hepburn and Tracy didn't make this movie until the early fifties," Luke commented.

"I know," Kealey replied confidently. "I've seen everything they've done—from their first film, *Woman of the Year.*"

Luke nodded. "You know, Katherine Hepburn wanted Tracy to star in *The Philadelphia Story* with her before that, but the studio chose Cary Grant."

Kealey's head swiveled toward him in surprise. "I didn't know that." She paused, her words a reluctant admission. "And I thought I knew a lot about them."

Luke's voice was casual, easy. It was obvious he enjoyed sharing the information; this was no attempt to impress her with the knowledge. "Actually, she'd never met Spencer Tracy, but she'd seen everything he had done and admired his work. So she bought the rights to *Woman of The Year,* went to Louis B. Mayer and offered him the script, along with herself as the female lead for the bargain price of $250,000. Her only stipulation was that Spencer Tracy be given the lead opposite her."

"Really?" she questioned, completely fascinated.

"Yep. She met Spencer Tracy on one of the side lots at MGM. She was a tall woman for that time, over five foot seven and she was wearing high heels. Tracy was about 5'10". When producer Joe Mankowitz introduced them, she said something like, 'Sorry I've got these high heels on, but when we do the movie I'll be careful about what I wear.'"

"And what did Tracy say?" Kealey promptly asked.

Luke smiled. "Apparently Tracy just looked at her with those great lion eyes of his. But Joe Mankowitz had something to say."

"What?" she urged.

"He said, 'Don't worry, Kate. He'll cut you down to his size.'"

"I wonder what Tracy really thought of her," Kealey mused.

"Katherine Hepburn said he thought she was peculiar at first."

Kealey's laugh was soft. "Hardly an auspicious beginning for what many people consider the romance of the last century."

"I don't know. They spent twenty-seven years together. And according to Katherine Hepburn, he made her understand for the first time what it meant to be in love."

She swallowed. "That's really beautiful. Hardly anyone stays together that long anymore."

Luke's arm rested lightly on her shoulders. "I don't know. It's pretty much a tradition in my family."

Of course it was. Feeling suddenly bereft, she couldn't offer a response. She had no traditions, no family, no belief in forever.

Luke began gently stroking her hair, his own quiet signaling that he didn't need or expect a reply. For a brief moment, her eyes drifted closed and she imagined what it would be like to sit beside this man for the next thirty or forty some odd years, to have these beautiful children's own children nestled by their feet.

As she wondered, the old movie continued to play, the familiar words and images a comfort. However, as she'd predicted, the children began nodding off. And before the movie ended, Luke started scooping up limp little bodies. With Kealey's help, he put them all to bed.

Brian and Troy were first. Tucked into twin beds, Luke made certain they were settled in, then switched on a discreet night-light that banished the utter darkness with a faint glow. Luke had confided that Brian still had a few lingering nightmares. Impulsively, Kealey bent over this oldest, bravest little soldier and kissed his forehead.

While Luke finished tucking in Troy, Kealey saw to Hannah in the next room. Tugging the blanket up over little Hannah, she felt a fierce longing in her heart to have these children for her very own.

Hearing Luke's quiet tread as he entered the room, she glanced up, trying to force away the longing. "They look awfully sweet when they're sleeping, don't they?" she whispered.

"They're not so bad awake, either," he whispered back.

They paused in the hallway outside Hannah's room. Hesitantly, Kealey glanced at Luke's bedroom, wondering if this was it.

He took her elbow, however, steering her toward the stairs. "We've got a movie to finish watching."

She swallowed, knowing there was little more than half an hour left of the film. But it was a reprieve.

Kealey was amazed, however, when the movie ended, and Luke withdrew another Hepburn-Tracy film video from a sack.

"Adam's Rib?"

He nodded. "Arguably their best."

"No. That would have to be *Keeper of The Flame*."

By then the credits were rolling, and they settled back on the couch, continuing to argue the merits of each film, pausing to appreciate the witty dialogue that hadn't dimmed over time, nibbling on popcorn from a shared bowl.

And without realizing how or when it happened, they slid closer together, laughing long and hard at the same things.

And the hours passed, one gliding into the next, the flames in the fireplace dimming to mere embers. Then, their eyes, too, began to droop....

SHE'D FORGOTTEN to close the drapes, Kealey thought sleepily. That's why the early-morning sunlight was stabbing at her eyes, forcing her to awaken. She reached to cover her eyes, but her hand wouldn't move; it seemed stuck.

With one eye open, she turned her head slightly.

But the other eye popped open when she realized the view wasn't from the bed in her own apartment. Instead, her face was pushed against Luke's chest. His muscular, broad chest.

Fascinated, she watched the even rise and fall of his breathing, allowing her gaze to travel up to his face, strongly tempted to trace the strong features.

They must have fallen asleep. Sometime between movies, popcorn and laughter, they'd drifted off. And now she was wound around Luke as though she belonged there.

Apparently sensing her gaze on him, Luke's eyes opened as well. And something unfathomable happened to the blue of his eyes, transforming them to near ebony as he continued to meet her gaze.

Kealey realized, somewhere in the last remaining fragments of her logic, that she should pull away, to disconnect their warm bodies. But Luke's eyes were still on hers.

He tilted his head, the angle putting his lips a breath away from hers. Instantly she remembered his kiss at their wedding ceremony, making her feel as if she were falling, connected to reality through what was only supposed to be a simple kiss.

She expected to again be kissed, but he spoke. "Good morning," he murmured, his voice low, husky, saturated with sleep…and perhaps something more.

Her gaze darted between his lips and eyes, and she felt her own mouth part as though it wanted to repeat that kiss. It was madness to long for what she'd hoped to postpone the previous evening.

But the debate in her mind stilled, when ever so gently his lips met hers. It was a tender exploration, a beckoning to something she hadn't even known was hidden beneath competency and loneliness.

For the first time, Kealey thought she could almost persuade herself that she was like all other women, that she could find security, perhaps even learn to trust. In the end, even the evoking promise of his lips couldn't make her really believe that.

Reluctantly, she drew back and saw disappointment dim his expression. She wanted to reverse her last motion, or at the least to explain why she'd withdrawn. But, that, too, wasn't in her.

To her surprise, instead of questioning her, Luke reached out, tucking back a few strands of hair that had fallen across her cheek. Shaken by his excruciatingly tender touch, she closed her eyes.

His words were filled with quiet understanding. "We have to get moving. The kids will be up soon and we'd better have breakfast going."

Her eyes opened. The kids. For a few minutes she'd forgotten about them. And they were the reason she'd suggested this entire arrangement. Moving away from Luke, she immediately missed the warm contact.

"How come you guys are sleeping on the couch?" Troy asked as he stumbled into the living room, wiping at his sleep-filled eyes.

"We got to watching movies," Luke explained.

"And stayed up past your bedtime?" Troy asked.

Kealey's eyes met Luke's, and amusement flowed between them.

"Guess you could say that," Luke replied, his lip twitching only marginally.

Kealey forced her thoughts away from Luke. "We were just saying we need to get breakfast going. Why don't you come help me make some orange juice?"

Troy nodded. "I like the stirring part."

Kealey stood, looping an arm around Troy's shoulder. "Then stirring it'll be. How do pancakes sound?"

"Yum. Chocolate chip?"

She ruffled his hair. "I don't think so. Not on a school day. I think we'll stick to blueberry." She glanced back at Luke, unable to completely conceal her longing. "It's just another day."

A FEW HOURS LATER, the children safely off to school, the dishes done, the house straightened, Kealey prepared to head back to her apartment. There hadn't been that much to do. Luke had been a self-sufficient bachelor, accustomed to keeping his home neat. And the kids had all made their beds and put away their things.

Kealey had taken a few days off from work, a novelty for her, and she needed to keep herself busy.

Collecting her purse and keys, she was surprised to see Luke coming out of his clinic.

"Good timing," he greeted her. "How about some lunch?"

"It's a little early for lunch," she hedged. "I'm going to my apartment to finish packing."

"I'll help," he replied.

"It's not necessary," she protested.

"You know I have Dr. Gates covering my practice," he told her. "I was just checking on our boarders. Besides, Wayne will be here if anything comes up while we're gone."

"But—"

"Didn't anyone ever tell you that you're a girl?"

She blinked. *"Girl?"*

"Woman, female, member of the gentler sex. One who could use some help with a few heavy boxes."

One brow lifted skeptically. "From a big, macho man like you?"

Despite the tone of her voice, he grinned. "Yes, *ma'am.*"

She rolled her eyes. "Another one of those Texas mannerisms?"

"Afraid so," he replied, taking her elbow, guiding her to the door. "We should probably take my Bronco. More room for the boxes."

Kealey opened her mouth to protest, then realized this man operated like a steamroller. "I'm sure you have a ton of things in the clinic you've wanted to catch up on. This is your opportunity."

He met her gaze, his own dark and a tad myste-rious. "I like to choose my own opportunities."

Unable to even begin to think of a reply, she al-lowed him to lead her to his car, then drive to her apartment. Even as she unlocked her front door, she couldn't believe he'd taken such complete control. That was something she'd never allowed—at least since she'd become an adult.

The apartment didn't look a lot different to Luke than before she'd begun to move out. It wasn't that it looked neglected, rather it lacked character. And he now suspected why.

"I got most of my clothes the other day," Kealey was saying.

He wandered into the kitchen. "Would you like me to pack the dishes, pots and pans?"

She seemed to be concentrating deeply. "I guess so. But really, you could leave me to this and just help me carry out the boxes in a few hours."

"Kealey?"

Finally she looked up, still not completely drawn out of her contemplation. "Hmmm?"

"Has it occurred to you that I might *want* to be here, with you?"

Apparently it hadn't. Flustered, she gestured vaguely with her hands.

But he didn't want to extend her discomfort. "Be-sides, I'm an expert at moving."

She managed a tentative smile. "I thought you'd stayed mostly in Greenville."

"Except for college and vet school, yes. But with seven siblings, it seems like someone's constantly moving. And being single Uncle Luke, I've always been drafted."

She stared at him.

His next words tumbled out quickly. "Formerly single Uncle Luke."

Kealey swallowed. "I don't want you to feel uncomfortable about that." She glanced down, tilting her head at an uncertain angle. "I don't expect you to think like a married man."

His own voice was quiet. "But I am a married man."

Her look beseeched him. "We don't have to make this more difficult than it already is."

"I don't know. I wasn't thinking it was especially difficult."

Her hands twisted, a telltale sign of nerves. "Well, I'm not casual and easygoing like you. I wish I were. I've always wished I could be like other people—taking things in stride, not tensing over the least little bit of nothing."

"Why would you wish that?" he asked, his voice still quiet.

Exasperated, she stared at him in silent rebuke. "How can you ask that? Doesn't everyone want to fit in?"

He studied her carefully. "I suppose. In some ways. But isn't it more important to be unique…special?"

Her voice grew strained, as though fighting bitterness and repressed tears. "I'm neither of those things."

He didn't know why. But he suddenly knew it was incredibly important to convince her how amazing she really was. "Oh, so just anyone cares enough about foster children to become a social worker?"

She stared at him suspiciously. "Your own sister's a social worker."

"And I happen to think she's a hell of a special person," he replied. "Your point?"

"Of course Rachel's special, but that doesn't mean—"

"That you are?"

Shadows mingled in the changing colors of her eyes. Blue darted past gray. "Look..." Her eyes closed briefly, hiding that spectacular color show. And when she opened them, it was hesitantly, as though wishing they could remain shut. "You don't have to do this."

"What? Point out that the average woman doesn't forego a social life and personal comfort to check on the cases she's assigned?"

"But a lot of social workers do that," Kealey protested.

"Do they marry a foster parent to make sure three small children aren't separated?"

Her eyes began to shimmer and she blinked while biting down on her lower lip.

"When did you learn that habit?" Gently he ran the back of one knuckle over the clenched lip. "Why did you have to learn not to cry, Kealey?"

She jerked back, the movement sudden and jarring. And for a moment they looked at each other in startled dismay.

Then she turned away, presenting her back, which was rigid, unapproachable. "I told you I really don't need any help here."

"Did you get enough boxes?" he asked, abruptly changing the direction of their conversation.

"Boxes?" She glanced around, as though expecting cardboard containers to sprout on the carpet. "Well, no, but—"

"I'll go get some boxes, newspapers and tape. Do you have Cokes in the fridge?"

"A few, I think," she replied, still looking distracted. "But you don't need—"

"It won't take me a minute. I have a friend who runs a little convenience store. He usually has a lot of extra boxes and an unending supply of old newspapers."

"Luke, I—"

"I'll be back in a few minutes." Despite the "don't touch" warning she was giving him, he reached forward, brushing a quick kiss across her cheek. Then he grinned. "You'll find I'm harder to get rid of than gum on tennis shoes."

Still looking dazed, she didn't reply.

Luke took advantage of the pause to dash out the

door. She could scream that she didn't need help at the top of her lungs. But he was certain that he'd never seen anyone who needed help more.

KEALEY GLANCED AROUND the small kitchen. It wouldn't take long to pack. And she'd just finished with the bathroom, the one room that had more paraphernalia than any other.

She heard a loud knock, then the sound of the front door opening. "Kealey, it's Luke," he called out. "Armed and ready to pack."

His joking words caused her to smile despite her qualms. "Armed and ready to pack?"

He came to the door of the kitchen, holding up a sack of pink foam peanuts. "These pretty much kill the dangerous image. Gunther thought we might need them. Between you and me I think he saw this as a great chance to unload his cache of shipping garbage."

"I really don't have that much to pack."

"Then we may have to make use of your apartment's Dumpster. I'm afraid we have enough material to pack up the White House."

Her smile grew despite herself. "Surely you're exaggerating."

"Oh, not the one in Washington," he replied nonchalantly. Then Luke lowered his voice to a confidential level. "By the way, here in Texas, we haven't really gotten over the notion that we're still an independent country." His voice rose back to normal. "At any rate, I was referring to the store on Main Street. One side carries men's clothing, the other women's. The owners are Edna and George White."

"So it's the White House," she concluded, her lips curving upward in an irrepressible grin.

"You got it."

"This *is* a strange nation," she replied, tongue in cheek. "All soft drinks are called Cokes. And the heart of your country's capital specializes in clothing. Any more surprises?"

His grin was at once amused and tantalizing, as was his uncommonly husky voice. "Oh, I think so."

Kealey cleared her throat. "Well, I got the bathroom all packed."

"Why don't we work on the kitchen next?" he suggested, his gaze still full of promise.

Kealey wanted to tell him that they could work in separate areas to get the job completed faster.

She intended to.

Within a few minutes, however, she was working with him to wrap her meager supply of dishes. It didn't take long to finish.

"What next?" Luke asked. "The living room?"

She glanced in that direction. "The furniture's all rented, except the television and VCR. I don't think anything else in there is mine." Glancing up, she saw sudden sympathy cloud his eyes. But she didn't need his pity. "With the hours I work, there's not a lot of time or need for knickknacks."

He nodded. "Does the phone still work?"

Exasperated, she glanced at him. "Do you always change subjects so abruptly?"

He smiled. "Only when I'm hungry. How about a pizza for lunch? We can stay here and pack, not have to go out."

Kealey had a sudden memory of endless lonely evenings when she'd considered ordering a pizza, then hadn't because it seemed so forlorn to order a small pizza for one. It was like going to the movies or a restaurant by herself. They just seemed to reinforce how alone she was. It was one of the reasons why she'd started watching videos, which was when she'd fallen in love with old movies.

Glancing up she met Luke's inquisitive gaze. "Sounds great." And it did, she realized. What did it matter that it was make-believe? Why not pretend, even for this short time, that she was part of a couple, a family, rather than terribly, singularly alone?

As they waited for the pizza, Luke carried the boxes from the kitchen out to his vehicle. Then they started packing Kealey's bedroom.

The pizza arrived and they agreed to remain settled in the middle of the bedroom floor, to eat as they packed. The mood was companionable, one that allowed her to trick him into eating an anchovy and one that allowed her to forget, for the moment, how temporary this all was.

Luke was packing her books. He turned one over

in his hands. "Most of these relate to your work. Don't you ever read for pleasure?"

Perplexed, she stared back at him. "My work is a pleasure for me."

His gaze was gentle, yet it seemed to probe deeply. "That's a fortunate thing for a lot of kids."

Inordinately pleased, she averted her gaze.

"But don't you think you deserve a little something for yourself?"

She glanced at him in question. "I have plenty."

His gaze wandered over her scant collection of belongings. "I don't want to pry, Kealey. I'm asking because I want to know about you, to understand why you seem to have so little in your life."

She took a deep breath, wishing she hadn't allowed herself to become so comfortable. "You know that I was a foster child." She shrugged as she stated the obvious. "Thus, no affluent background. Because I'd been part of the foster system I simply became a social worker, so I don't deserve your praise for that decision."

"You suffered and knowing how that felt, you're trying to prevent others from suffering. Sorry, but that still makes you special."

She bit her lip again. How was this man able to say things that hit every well-hidden target?

His voice gentled even further. "Even though you were in the foster system, weren't you able to keep any special mementos?"

"From what?" Kealey asked, acceptance dulling any lingering bitterness.

"Didn't you like your foster parents?"

"I got moved around a lot." She sighed, a heart-felt sound that echoed around them. "That's why I was…why I *am* convinced a two-parent home is better for children. Unless both parents are deficient, the kids have better odds than one-on-one with a single adult."

"You had bad single foster parents?"

She hesitated. There was no easy answer. Surely no short one. "Let's just say that I know what that experience is all about, firsthand."

"Is that why you went above and beyond for our kids?"

Our kids? Is that how he really thought about them? And then there were her feelings for Luke, ones she knew she could never express…

"Whatever the reason," he answered for her. "They're lucky kids."

Kealey shrugged. "I'm the lucky one. They're great kids, ones who deserve a future." Finally she met his gaze. "And they'll get that with you."

"I'm guessing that's a pretty big compliment, considering your conviction about two-parent homes."

"Sometimes," she began hesitantly, still feeling the sting of her error in judgment, "I become so convinced of certain things that I refuse to look for the exception until it's too late."

Luke shrugged. "I don't know. I've tried to put myself in your place. You walk into a house crowded with kids, animals and an entire pack of relatives. And then you come face-to-face with the jerk who took you on a blind date and didn't have enough sense to realize he was with someone pretty special."

Ridiculously, her eyes began to moisten and raw emotion lodged in her throat.

"And even then, when the jerk began to berate you, you kept the best interest of the children in mind. Most people would have snatched away the kids, leaving me in the dust, wishing I'd had either good sense or at least good manners."

Kealey started to bite down on her lip again. But Luke was faster, his thumb caressing her lower lip, blocking her access to it.

Then his mouth closed over hers.

Again she sensed the questioning in his kiss. But the feeling that lingered long after the kiss was his excruciating tenderness. And that, she knew, would be the most difficult to forget.

CHAPTER TWELVE

THE STRAY LOOKED horrible, not just dirty and underfed, but as though something was terribly wrong with him. Brian was gazing at Luke with hope, no doubt sure that his new hero and father couldn't fail him. Kealey was looking at Luke with equal trepidation.

"You can fix him, can't you, Luke?" Brian was asking, his voice a plea.

Luke's large hands probed gently over the gray dog's abdomen. "You found him by the side of the road?"

"Uh-huh," Brian bobbed his head up and down earnestly. "Just to the side on the gravel part. He looked like he was asleep, 'cept he was making a funny kind of noise. He wouldn't get up, so I had to bring him home in Troy's wagon."

Luke's face was sober. "Brian, I'm going to do my best with him, but he's in pretty bad shape."

"But you fix all kinds of sick animals!" Brian protested.

"I know, but this one's hurt badly. It looks as though he was hit by a car. I'll run X rays and get him into surgery right away, but he may not make it.''

Brian's eyes widened in shock as he stared at Luke in disbelief.

Luke stood up, meeting Kealey's eyes. ''Could you take Brian into the house?''

''But we could stay and help—'' Brian started to protest.

''Wayne and I will do our best,'' Luke replied, his voice compassionate but firm. ''And to do that we'll need everyone out of our way.''

Kealey put her hand on Brian's shoulder. ''Let's go make some cookies for your brother and sister. It'll make the time go faster.''

ALTHOUGH THEY MADE several batches of cookies, the time still crawled by. Troy and Hannah, filled in on the emergency, sat quietly beside their brother.

None of them had even tasted one of the dozens of cookies. She should take them to a shelter, Kealey thought inanely, so they didn't go to waste.

Luke pushed open the kitchen door at that moment and she and the kids took a collective breath.

Luke looked only at Brian.

And Kealey knew at that instant the news was as bad as she'd suspected.

Brian ran over to Luke, his gaze filled with both fear and hope. ''Is he okay?''

Luke's face, sober and drawn, tightened even

more as he knelt down beside him. "I'm afraid not."

Brian stared at him as though by doing so Luke would change his reply. "He's really..."

Luke nodded. "I'm sorry, son. I wish I could have done better."

Brian's eyes started to fill.

Instinctively, Luke drew him close, Brian's head resting on his shoulder as the tears escaped.

Hannah and Troy looked at their brother and then Kealey. She took both their hands and they watched silently as their brother grieved.

Minutes later, Brian lifted his head. He and Luke exchanged a few quiet words, ones Kealey and the other children couldn't hear. When Brian's tears finally ceased, Luke stood, keeping his arm around the boy's shoulders.

Together they faced the others as Luke spoke. "Brian has agreed that we should have a funeral in the backyard now."

Hannah and Troy nodded soberly.

Quietly, they all filed out the back door. Wayne stood to one side of a freshly dug grave. No doubt he'd been hard at work while Luke broke the news. Kealey saw Luke's wooden tool crate had been taken from the garage. Apparently it had been hastily emptied to provide a makeshift coffin.

"Is the dog inside?" Hannah whispered.

Luke nodded, then tightened his grip on Brian's shoulder. "We wrapped him in a blanket first."

"So he'll be warm," Hannah said.

Kealey met Luke's eyes. There would be no more warmth for this poor animal. Keeping her voice low, she questioned him. "Did the dog have a collar?"

Luke shook his head. "He was clearly a stray."

They gathered around the small pile of upturned earth.

Luke still stood beside Brian. "I think we should say a few words over this dog. Sadly, we never knew his name or if he had a home at one time. But he's one of God's creatures, one who deserves our care and respect. While he hasn't had a home for some time, perhaps never did, he was not without fortune. Because someone did care. Young Brian Baker cared enough to rescue him from a cold and lonely end. For a brief time he had a champion, and now he'll rest in our yard, and we'll remember him, and how he touched our lives."

There was quiet after Luke's words and Brian swiped at the tears still lingering in his eyes.

Then Luke asked Brian, "Do you want to say something?"

Slowly Brian nodded. "I'm sorry we didn't get to know you, dog. You would have liked Luke, cause he cares about dogs and kids and anybody else that don't have a home. And like he said, we'll remember you and maybe our mama can make sure you're okay in Heaven."

Kealey hadn't realized her tears had started until her cheeks were wet and her vision blurred. Unable to wipe them away without releasing Troy and Hannah's hands, she willed them away, yet they continued to slide relentlessly down her face. She knew she was crying for more than this dog. She was crying for all strays like herself, the children who were thrust daily into an overcrowded foster system with no one like Luke to care or make a difference.

At a nod from Luke, Wayne picked up the wooden box and placed it gently in the grave. Then he walked over to the shovel, holding it out to Brian. "The first shovelful should be yours."

Brian looked up at Luke for confirmation, then accepted the shovel. He pitched the newly turned soil onto the box, his voice barely audible. "Goodbye, little dog."

Then, one by one, they each took their turns. Luke was last. He then handed the shovel to Wayne, who had apparently agreed to complete the burial once the kids were inside.

Kealey couldn't resist one last look over her shoulder as they walked into the house. The grave didn't seem as sad and forlorn surrounded by the quiet beauty of Luke's yard.

Still, once in the kitchen, the kids were quiet. Although Kealey tempted them with hot dogs, no one ate much. Homework was completed in near silence. One by one, the kids began to troop upstairs. Brian was the last. As Kealey stood in the kitchen, he paused on the first riser. Swiftly he turned back around, reaching up to hug Luke. Then he ran up the stairs.

Unaware that she was watching, Luke's face was a swarm of emotions. It was the first time she'd seen him look vulnerable, defeated. And the love that she had for him swelled.

The next few hours passed quietly. Luke was deep in thought, his face somber, and Kealey was awash in reflections of her own.

The night lengthened and he finally stood. "I'll say good-night."

She swallowed, smothering her doubts. "I'll come upstairs now, too."

He looked at her in surprise, but nodded, reaching to flip off the lights.

It was unlike her, Kealey knew. She'd made excuses to stay up later, then crept up the stairs to stealthily climb into the bed. Then she would hang on to the edge of her side of the bed, keeping as much space as possible between them, not relaxing until she finally heard the change in Luke's breathing that told her he was asleep.

Always an early riser, she made sure she was up and out of the room before he was. She probably would have risen at 3:00 a.m. if it had been necessary.

Never before had she accompanied him up the stairs, with the darkness of the first floor disappearing beneath them. But never before had she felt such need to make someone believe again in himself.

Inside the bedroom, her jitters returned. Her glance darted around the room, resting on her portion of the dresser. It didn't look at all like she'd left it that morning.

Slowly she crossed the room, fingering the antique dresser set, a tortoiseshell comb, brush and mirror. She glanced over at Luke. "Where did this come from?"

Still deep in thought, he glanced up and saw her holding the boar-bristle brush. "I thought you might like it."

Fingers tentative, nearly shaking, she stroked the beautiful amber-colored pieces. "But..."

"It's a little thing, Kealey, and I thought it suited you. The colors change under different lights— much like your eyes."

"It's not my birthday or—"

"It doesn't have to be," he interrupted quietly. "Sometimes, people need to give just for the joy of giving."

Slowly she nodded, overcome by his thoughtfulness. He'd been giving her inexpensive little gifts since the day he'd learned she owned virtually nothing. It was as though he were building a cache that she could claim as her own. Combined with how she was already feeling about his behavior that day, she couldn't speak.

But he was very right, sometimes a person needed to give—just as she did right now. She needed to offer him comfort, to prove he was still their hero.

Luke shrugged off his T-shirt and kicked away his jeans. Mesmerized, Kealey stood in front of the dresser mirror watching him. Well-defined muscles, so firm they didn't even ripple, covered his chest, arms and legs. His perfectly tapered torso looked as though it belonged on a male model. But the masculine features of his face were far too rugged.

They were meant to appeal to women.

And they did.

Quietly, she collected her nightgown, escaping into the bathroom to change. Gazing into the mirror, she searched her own eyes, trying to see what Luke did. Unable to see beyond her uncertainty and neediness, she looked away. Still, she remembered *his* need, the only need left unattended since he was always giving to others.

Luke had left one lamp on in the room, the one on her nightstand, the one he'd added just for her. The dim glow illuminated the bed. With shaky hands, she turned off the light. And in the sudden darkness the click echoed, unbelievably loud. The only sound in the room, Kealey realized. Luke's breathing was quiet, controlled. He had to be awake.

Inhaling a deep breath of her own, she eased onto the bed. The sheets were cool, not the icy cold of winter, but refreshingly cool. Inhaling, she could smell the faint tang of his cologne, the subtle aroma of his soap.

She slid closer to the middle of the bed. Closer to Luke.

And his breathing changed.

It wasn't transforming into the rhythm of sleep, however. It had quickened, deepened.

For a moment she froze.

But her instincts told her it wasn't the time to back down, to run away.

She inched over another millimeter. Then another.

Just as she was gathering her courage, Luke flipped from his back to his side. Before she could think, his face was next to hers, his body within a handspan.

"Kealey?" he questioned, baffled, intrigued, tempted.

Somewhere between his inquiry and her answer, she reached out, tentatively touching his chest. Her fingers trembled, then spread against his skin. To her amazement, the skin covering his muscles felt like velvet. But then nothing about Luke had ever been rough. Strong, but not rough.

And it was that gentle strength that he reached out with, his arms drawing her close to him. Swallowing, Kealey kept her gaze on his as he stroked her hair, then kissed the most tender skin of her neck. The kisses were gentle nibbles that started somewhere near her throat and traveled in slow succession to the underside of her chin.

Then the butterfly kisses touched her eyelids, whispered along her cheek and captured her lips. It wasn't so much one eruption; rather it was the constant explosion of a fireworks display.

His hands caressed her shoulders, pushing down the straps of her willowy gown. The air teased her bared skin as did the whisper of his breath as it traced her silhouette. How could a touch so light, so sure, create such immense sensation?

And how could she be so ready to fall headlong and helpless into this man's embrace? Even as she wondered, he sketched the contours of her rib cage, pausing at the indentation of her waist, lingering over the slope of her hips, then walking his fingers down the length of her thigh.

Somehow she remembered to breathe. As he retraced the path upward, his gaze again met and held hers. And before he lowered his mouth to hers, he extracted an unspoken promise, one that said she was aware, certain, that this would not be a solitary act, nor one born of mere physical need. And she, Kealey Fitzpatrick, disbeliever of all promises, silently believed.

Limbs somehow entangled themselves, skin sought skin, lips encountered, challenged, gasped and encountered again.

His hands smoothed the hair back from her face and she felt the power of his gaze, the intensity of his touch. And she fell in love with him all over again.

Luke cupped her head in his hands, unable to believe this was his Kealey. *His* Kealey? As if that could possibly be.

Yet even now her fragile but potent touch was

sending him rocketing into an orbit he hadn't known existed.

Closing his eyes, he remembered the agony of the day and knew this was her gift, her quiet show of support and belief.

Chasing away the thoughts, she nipped gently on his earlobe, her voice a siren's murmur, her rapid heartbeat a thrumming call. But it was the expression in her eyes that vaulted past excitement and treaded on his heart.

He had seen her tears that day, had glimpsed part of her he'd never seen before. And that was why he'd made sure she was ready to take this step. He sensed without being told that she'd suffered great pain in her life. He didn't want to add to it.

She reached up just then, caressing his jaw. Capturing her hand, he kissed each finger, exulting in her sighs of pleasure.

Then he was cradling her body, her cries lost in his own.

CHAPTER THIRTEEN

KEALEY PUSHED ASIDE a growing stack of case files. The numbers were discouraging, but then the cases never decreased. However, every once in a while, like today, she was able to be a part of placing a child in a permanent home. A safe, loving home with wonderful people who were thrilled to have a five-year-old boy to complete their family.

"Hey, Kealey, nice job today," Rachel greeted her.

Kealey smiled, remembering the adoption that morning, the hugs that filled the courtroom. "It was great. I just wish they could all turn out that way."

Rachel nodded. It was something every social worker hoped and worked for. "Well, it looks like your batting average is up today."

Kealey looked at her in question.

Rachel handed her a message slip. "You got a call from Aging Services about the senior dog adoption. They think they've found your first candidate."

Kealey smiled thoughtfully. "The kids could really use this news right now, especially Brian. This past week they've all been down."

Rachel nodded, having heard the unfortunate

story of the stray Luke hadn't been able to save. "I guess he took it the hardest."

"Actually I think Luke really took it to heart."

"He would. He's always been the protector, the rescuer."

Kealey idly fingered the smallish piece of paper. "I think he believes he failed the kids, let them down."

Rachel nodded. "Even my big brother can't win every time." Her gaze softened. "Although I think this time he did."

Puzzled, Kealey glanced at her. "He did?"

"With you. Between the two of you, you're helping a lot of people." She glanced down at the pink message slip. "And animals. Sounds like a pretty good partnership to me."

Kealey tried to wave away the words.

Rachel, however, only smiled. "Protest all you like. But remember. I'm a hardened social worker, takes a lot to convince me." Leaving her friend openmouthed, Rachel strolled away.

It took Kealey a moment to recover, then she glanced down at the message slip. Fingers crossed, she began her calls. Maybe, just maybe, she could coordinate this. It would be absolutely miraculous to begin and end the day with good news.

MRS. CONRAD WAS a tiny slip of a woman. Her hair resembled silver cotton candy, and her bright-blue eyes were filled with intelligence and kindness.

Her cozy home was tidy but filled with a lifetime of memories—family pictures, a treasured collection of porcelain figurines and an assortment of intriguing objects that looked faintly exotic. She had collected them when she'd traveled, she explained, when her husband was still alive. She was alone—they hadn't been blessed with children—and the photos were of relatives now gone.

She ushered them in warmly, taking time to speak to each child, to learn a little about them. But when Luke suggested he bring in the dog they'd brought, her interest visibly peaked.

Kealey glanced at the children's expectant faces and crossed her fingers. She desperately hoped she hadn't made a mistake in pushing this suggestion. Another defeat so soon would be a disaster.

Luke returned a few moments later, leading the old Border collie on a sturdy leather leash.

Mrs. Conrad's eyes brightened as she studied the dog. "He looks remarkably like my Mackie," she marveled in a near whisper. "And I've missed him so much."

Luke unhooked the leash and they all took a collective breath.

The medium-size black-and-white dog studied the room, sniffed the air and then made his slow way over to Mrs. Conrad. Her eyes filled again as she reached arthritic hands toward his muzzle. "Well hello, you."

As though returning to a long-lost mistress, the dog laid his head in her lap.

The kids stared in wonder. Kealey's gaze lifted to meet Luke's. There she saw approval…and so very much more.

"It's like having an old friend come back home. Can he really be mine?" Mrs. Conrad asked, wiping her eyes with a lace-edged handkerchief.

"If you'd like for him to be," Luke replied. "As Kealey told you, he's an older dog."

Mrs. Conrad's gaze was discerning. "I couldn't handle a young pup. They have so much energy and need long walks and someone who can really play with them. That's why I didn't get another pet after my Mackie…" She paused, then petted the Border collie. "It looks as though this one and I go about the same speed."

Kealey finally smiled. "You do seem like a good match."

Mrs. Conrad smiled as well. "What's his name?"

"We're not real sure," Brian replied. "We thought maybe you might want to name him."

"I think I'd like that," Mrs. Conrad answered softly. Then she glanced up. "Do I pay an adoption fee?"

Luke shook his head. "You've enriched us, just knowing what a fine home this dog will have. He has a license. It's on his collar and all his shots are up-to-date." He walked over to her, handing her a card. "If he needs any medical care, or just routine shots, call me. We'll come pick him up and take care of him.''

"I *am* on a fixed income, but I do like to pay my way,'' she told them, concern pulling the smile from her face.

"Mrs. Conrad, we can't possibly repay you for giving him a loving home. Few people would accept an elderly dog. Providing medical care is the least I can do to repay you,'' Luke told her in all seriousness.

Her smile slowly returned. "You're an exceptional young man.'' Then she glanced down at the Border collie. "And you're right, we senior citizens have to stick together.'' Then her gaze lifted to include them all. "What a special family you are.''

Kealey's gaze collided with Luke's and she couldn't look away.

Mrs. Conrad's soft voice had paused, but now she spoke again. "I think a dog's name should be meaningful, filled with character. So I believe I will call my new friend Duncan, if that's all right with you.''

Luke was the first to speak. "It would be an honor.'' He turned to include the kids. "Right?''

Beaming smiles covered their faces. One by one they bid Duncan goodbye, offering pats, kisses and murmurs of how much they would miss him.

After they'd climbed back into Luke's SUV and buckled in, Kealey turned to assess their expressions. Hannah and Troy looked cheery, Brian thoughtful.

"You okay?" she asked him quietly.

"Uh-huh. I kind of miss him."

"That's natural. It's when we don't miss those who go away that we should worry. He looked pretty happy to be with Mrs. Conrad."

"She was nice, huh?"

"Very." Kealey hesitated. "And I think she needed him more than we do."

"So she wouldn't be alone?"

"Exactly. We have Bentley, Miles, Ginger, Kate, Spencer and Miss Tansy."

Brian seemed to consider this. "Dogs make good friends."

"Like Bentley?" she asked softly.

He finally smiled. "Yeah, he's the best."

She smiled, too. "That's how Miss Conrad's going to feel about Duncan."

"Then that's good," he decided.

Turning back around, she realized Luke's attention was on her. "Are you happy about the match we just made?" she asked anxiously.

His grin made Mrs. Conrad's smile dim in comparison. "*You* did great. I thought I was pretty good at placing strays, but you've become an expert."

She tried to demur.

"Face it. You're an expert with kids *and* animals."

Inexplicably pleased, Kealey didn't know how to respond.

But Luke didn't seem to need an answer. Instead,

he placed one hand on her knee. His touch conveyed both comfort and a spark of shared pleasure.

When he took his gaze off the road for a moment, she could read what he was thinking—about the previous night's passion. It seemed hard to believe that each night escalated beyond the last.

Luke dragged his attention back to the small bit of traffic on the road. "I feel like celebrating." He met her questioning look. "About Duncan and all. Do you feel like having dinner out?"

Kealey thought about the briefcase full of paperwork she'd brought home and for the first time in her career, decided it could wait. "Sure."

Luke raised his voice, calling out to the kids. "How about going to Buck's for dinner?"

Cheers greeted his words. Kealey couldn't repress a smile. Luke could suggest sardines on a hard rock in the freezing cold and they'd think it was wonderful because it was his idea.

"Buck's Tavern?" she asked him, vaguely remembering an old Western ranch house with that name.

"Best barbecue this side of Dallas. They have a long-neck beer bar, a sawdust dance floor, and a jukebox filled with country-and-western tunes that are older than we are. Not too uptown, but it's real family friendly. Kind of the Texas version of a pub except they serve Lone Star beer instead of ale."

She smiled, unaware that she was doing more and more of that these days. When he returned it with a grin of his own, the warm spot that was growing inside took another giant step forward.

It didn't take long to reach Buck's, even less time to order and receive their food.

She took a bite of her barbecue beef sandwich, prepared to make a polite comment. But the taste of the juicy, slow-cooked, mesquite-grilled meat silenced her.

"And you thought it was just another sandwich," Luke told her in a voice filled with knowing laughter.

"I'm a believer now," she responded. "How is it you know about every little restaurant in town?"

"I've lived here forever," he reminded her. When she automatically began to close up, he reached for her hand. "But anyone can learn. Especially with the right guide. And it won't take forever to make you feel like a native, too."

"It won't?" she asked, unable to hide the shakiness in her voice...or her heart.

"Nah." He played with the gold band on her left hand. "Sometimes it's part of the package deal."

Hope, that had been blossoming for months, beat frantically against the walls of her chest. Could she start believing that there might be a forever for them? Remembered pain burst through the hope. Glancing at Luke and the children, she realized that they deserved more. They deserved someone as unscarred as Luke himself.

She was quiet as they finished their sandwiches.

The waitress brought over dishes of homemade peach cobbler with generous scoops of ice cream. Even though it was delicious, she only took a few small bites. Someone plunked more quarters in the jukebox and a soft tune about lost love began to play.

Luke pushed aside his dessert. ''That dance floor looks downright abandoned. Want to help me do something about that?''

Kealey didn't know which was worse. To be held in his arms, or to wish to be there. She raised her chin. Their relationship might be short-term, but why should she deny herself the pleasure of this brief time? Standing, she allowed him to lead her onto the scarred wooden floor.

Her head fit naturally against his shoulder and their hips aligned perfectly as their legs moved in unison.

Luke inhaled the sweet, feminine smell of her soft hair. Soft hair, soft skin...possibly a soft heart? Although he relished their nights of passion, she'd yet to loosen the tight lock on her heart.

He worried that once the adoption was in place, she would walk away. Unable to believe in permanence, promises or security, Kealey had no use for love in any of its forms.

When they had entered their agreement, he'd thought she would come around, modify her unyielding views. She had, however, changed only marginally. And that seemed to be without her realization. Her past was a barricade he wasn't certain any man could conquer.

They turned in step to the music and she lifted her head to meet his gaze. Her eyes were doing that mysterious changing thing again, drifting from gray to sapphire. It reminded him of the sky meeting the ocean, the turbulence, the force. And in their stormy centers, he glimpsed that vulnerability she almost never exposed.

And it shot straight to his heart.

In the old dusky tavern he knew he loved her. Every ornery, rigid, uptight, scarred inch of her. Perhaps it was the scars he loved the most, the ones that made her give her life to children she didn't even know and scrounge up homes for animals she'd never before seen. All of which made her appear as though she would give the world to be able to trust.

The realization nearly made him stumble. Her arms tightened around him protectively. "It's the floor, it's not very even," she told him, obviously not wanting him to be worried about the fumble.

How could she not see the concern that seeped from her very pores? It was who she was, why she made the world a better place.

Kealey leaned her head back, offering a reassuring smile. "It's a nice song, isn't it?"

He hadn't a clue what the jukebox was playing. Moving by instinct alone, he wasn't thinking about the music. Still he nodded as the tune faded away. But he didn't release her.

She cleared her throat. ''I think the song's over.''

''Another will play,'' he replied, thinking he would feed the jukebox for hours if need be.

She searched his face, but he wasn't ready to tell her how he felt. Instinctively, he guessed the truth would scare her away. She'd heard too many empty promises in her life.

Then it hit him, another truth nearly as agonizing as the first. How would he ever convince her?

The music continued playing, by turns slow and easy, then gut-wrenching and woeful. Against all reason, she melted into his arms. And he took the moment, knowing there would be few enough of them in which to win her trust. If that was ever to be.

CHAPTER FOURTEEN

IT WAS ONLY a child's birthday party, but Kealey was inexplicably nervous as she helped Hannah dress. The little girl alternately stood patiently and danced up on her toes in anticipation.

Kealey had primped and fluffed Hannah's hair and then primped some more. Now she was retying the bow on Hannah's frilly dress for the third time. It was a beautiful party dress. Flowered organza and ivory lace tiered over a starched, full underskirt. Kealey had made certain the ivory tights matched exactly. And Hannah's black Mary Janes were nearly as shiny and bright as her excited eyes.

"I can't wait for the party to start," Hannah told her. "I haven't been invited to a dress-up party before."

Kealey's throat worked. She could see so much of herself in Hannah. And she could remember being the same age, seeing the other girls in school being invited to parties, but her invitation never arrived. She was the foster kid—the odd one out in every class. Kealey couldn't halt a flood of memories—longing to belong, to have a home and parents and parties. Things all the other kids took for granted. Kealey desperately wanted Hannah, Brian and Troy to have all those things.

And in the time since she and Luke had married she had been accumulating special little things for all of them. It wasn't a conscious decision, but there was the pair of expensive and distinctive tennis shoes along with equally extravagant jeans for Brian just so that he could fit in with the other boys.

And she'd bought Troy a monster toy complex he'd been eyeing, along with all the accessories.

With Hannah, she'd gone a little overboard, finding herself purchasing many of the things she'd wanted for herself as a girl. And she couldn't resist this last gift, a precious little necklace that was perfect with the new dress.

With the necklace fastened, Hannah spun around, pausing so that Kealey could straighten the center heart. "I wish you could stay my mommy always."

Nonplussed, Kealey's fingers halted midmotion. "Always?"

"Like Luke's going to be our dad," Hannah explained.

Kealey swallowed against the longing choking her. "You understood what we told you before the wedding, didn't you, sweetie? About our marriage ending when the adoption's final?"

"Uh-huh. But I was just wishing…"

Closing her eyes, Kealey hugged Hannah close for a moment. Then, although she wanted to hold on to the child forever, she purposely distracted her. "So, you really like the necklace?"

Hannah fingered the trinket. "It's *so* pretty!" she exclaimed for the dozenth time.

Kealey smiled, old memories fading, covered by these new ones. "And it looks perfect on you."

Hannah peered at the mirror. "Do I really look okay?"

Kealey shook her head. "Nope. You look lots more than okay. You look very pretty."

Hannah flung her arms around Kealey's neck. "Pretty like you?"

Kealey's eyes misted. How very precious this child was. "Much, much prettier."

Then she heard a distinctive cough from the doorway. Together, she and Hannah looked up to see Luke leaning against the door frame, watching them.

"If you ask me, you both look smashing," he said with a wink.

Hannah giggled.

Absurdly, Kealey felt the heat of a blush crawling up her neck, warming her face.

Then Luke drew his brows together. "Kealey, are you sure we should let Hannah go to this party?"

Kealey and Hannah looked at him with matching dismay.

"If Hannah goes," he continued, "won't all the other girls be jealous because she's the prettiest one there?"

Relieved, Hannah laughed. "Oh, Luke!"

Oh, Luke, indeed. Kealey managed to breathe again, not realizing until just then how important the child's happiness was to her.

To still the fluttering in her stomach, Kealey fussed again with Hannah's bow. Then she remembered the present she and Hannah had picked out for the birthday girl.

As she retrieved it, she noticed the pensive expression on Hannah's face. "Is something wrong, sweetie?"

"I wish Brian could come to the party."

"The party's only for girls," Kealey reminded her.

"I know, I just wish…"

Kealey tilted her head, studying Hannah's face.

Luke, too, moved closer. "Why just Brian? Not Troy, too?"

Hannah shook her head. "No, it's just that…"

Kealey's voice softened. "What is it?"

Hannah pushed her toe of her shiny party shoe into the nap of the rug. "Just that Brian didn't have a birthday this year."

Confused, Kealey glanced up at Luke.

"How could he not have a birthday?" Luke asked.

"It was about a week after Mama died and…"

Luke and Kealey looked at each other with horror on their faces. Although they'd glanced at the birthdays noted in the official files, amid all the confusion and controversy about placing the children, the timing of Brian's birthday hadn't occurred to either of them.

Kealey's gaze implored Luke to go along with her suggestion as she turned her attention back to Hannah. "Tell you what. We'll give Brian his own birthday party."

"But it's not his birthday," Hannah protested.

Kealey frantically searched her mind. "No. But it could be his half-year birthday."

"With balloons, cake and ice cream," Luke added. "But it should be a surprise, so you're going to have to keep this a secret until next Saturday."

"A whole *week?*" she wailed, as though they'd suggested a year rather than seven days.

"But you'll be helping us with the planning," Luke told her. "So you can talk to Kealey or me about it."

Hannah's brows drew together. "What about Troy?"

"How about if we wait until the end of the week to tell him? After all, he's a year younger than you and he may not be quite as able to keep a secret," Kealey replied.

Hannah considered this. "Okay." She seemed rather pleased at knowing such a secret. "This is the bestest time ever. A dress-up party *and* a secret." She reached up to hug first Kealey and then Luke.

Voice hoarse, Kealey agreed. "Yes, it is. Now, why don't you go downstairs. I'll be there in a minute."

Hannah skipped to the door, then the tapping of her dress shoes echoed down the wooden stairs.

"Oh, Luke," Kealey sighed.

"A ten-year-old boy loses his mother and has his birthday alone for the first time...and all in a single week."

She hesitated. "I hope my suggestion for a party was okay."

He cupped her chin. "As you told Hannah about her appearance, it's not okay. It's great."

Her smile was wobbly. "They're a surprise every day, aren't they, in some way or another?"

Luke nodded. "I keep thinking I'm getting used to them. Then a zinger like this one hits..."

She studied him in surprise. "But you seem to take it all in stride."

"And you seem in total control all the time. Could it be we're both wrong?"

Kealey swallowed. She could tell him so much, confide her longings, her hopes, even her dreams. But it still wasn't in her. So she began to edge toward the doorway. "I have to take Hannah to the party."

Although he nodded, Kealey knew he realized she was escaping. Despite that, she fled.

A WEEK OF keeping secrets, of all sorts, drove both Luke and Kealey crazy. After bringing Troy in on the surprise early Saturday morning, Luke promptly shipped him off to Mary's house before he could spill the news to Brian.

Later, Luke's parents stopped by, with the suggestion that Brian accompany them on a shopping excursion. Luckily, since Hannah was about to burst with the weight of her week-long secret, Luke's family began arriving soon afterward to help decorate and set up the party. Within a short time, the house and backyard began to radiate under an onslaught of streamers, balloons and banners.

Mary had baked a gigantic, elaborate cake in the shape of a sports car that was at least four layers deep with a good-size toy driver at the wheel. It was one of a kind and sure to make Brian's eyes pop when he saw it.

Luke's brother, Peter, nailed a piñata to one tree while Matt hung an old-fashioned pin-the-tail-on-the-donkey game on another. Between the siblings, they'd brought enough games and amusements for a mini carnival.

Kealey's breath caught when she saw Rachel's contribution—a giant, hugely lettered banner proclaiming Happy Birthday, Brian! When he arrived back home, there would be no mistaking this celebration was strictly for him.

Catching Luke's gaze across the yard, they shared a spontaneous grin. Just then the assigned lookout signaled that Brian had returned.

It was amazing that such a big crowd of people could quiet instantly. At the signal, the only sounds that could be heard in the backyard were the gentle swish of the balloons and streamers in the mild breeze.

The murmur of Brian's, Jane's and Timothy's voices drifted over the fence. Then the gate creaked open.

As soon as Brian crossed into the yard, all the voices shouted in unison. "Surprise!"

Stunned, Brian looked around at the smiling faces. Then his gaze landed on the banner. His gaze lifted to Luke's. "But it's not my birthday."

Luke winked at him. "I think Kealey has an explanation for that."

Tremulously, she smiled at this child, one who'd borne so much pain, who needed so desperately to simply be a child. "It's your half-year birthday, Brian."

His eyes widened in more surprise. "My half-year birthday?"

Kealey nodded. "It's sort of a rule, if you don't celebrate your birthday on the right day, you get a half-year party."

Glancing around the yard again, Brian looked overwhelmed. He blinked his eyes. Hard. His voice was hoarse, low. "Wow."

The single word warmed Kealey's heart in a way she hadn't known it could. Feeling Luke's gaze on hers, she lifted her eyes to meet his. Before she could anticipate his intention, he reached over and gently kissed her. The soft touch of his lips was a surprise…but more, an affirmation.

And part of her mind acknowledged that he'd kissed her in front of his entire family. And a beat later, she realized no one had taken much notice.

Then Brian was walking forward, surrounded by his loving, surrogate family.

"Come on," Luke was saying, taking Kealey's elbow, leading her into the midst of the group. "We don't want to miss the fun."

Initially, Brian was overcome by all the attention, but little by little, he relaxed. As he got into the spirit of the party, a full-blown overwhelming grin none of them had ever seen, bloomed. And in that instant he was all child again.

Soon, Brian, and his brother and sister, along with all the nieces and nephews, were involved in the games.

About an hour into the party, Jane approached Kealey and Luke. "There's a delivery here for you."

Luke started to step forward.

"For both of you," Jane added wryly.

Kealey and Luke exchanged puzzled glances, but followed Jane to the gate. Stepping outside, they both halted, their gazes going first to the curious-looking party clown, and then to the man dressed in cowboy gear who was holding the lead to a pony.

"You got a pony?" Luke asked, stunned.

"You got a clown?" she replied in equal surprise.

Jane rolled her eyes, her voice still wry. "If I've said it once, I've said it a hundred times, the number one rule in marriage is good communication."

Shock held Luke and Kealey still, then they both burst into laughter. It was a rare unaccustomed moment of pure joy for Kealey. And Luke was mesmerized by the genuine pleasure that captured her face.

Laughter spent, they turned again to their dual surprises, deciding this time to discuss how to accommodate both side shows. While the clown entertained part of the crowd on one side of the yard, a portion of the kids could line up for pony rides.

"So you rented a pony," Luke commented in a satisfied voice, after the entertainment was organized.

She bit down on her lip, finally saying wryly, "It was an impulse."

"*You* have impulses?" he asked.

Exasperated, she pushed back at the hair on her forehead. "Don't make such a big deal out of it."

"Me?" he asked in mock surprise. "Would I do that?"

She narrowed her eyes. "I'm not quite certain exactly *what* you'll do."

Laughter erupted from him. "No, you don't, do you?"

She studied him suspiciously. "You don't have another surprise planned, do you?"

His face drew into a reasonable semblance of seriousness—unless she noticed the twinkle in his eyes. "Now, if I told you that, it wouldn't be a surprise, would it?"

Her mind went through the possibilities, logic slowly giving way to the realization that he was teasing her. It was a novel experience for her. As a child so-called teasing by the other kids was more like restrained torture. She hadn't known it could be fun, with kind intentions.

On the other hand, she'd always been a quick study. Her smile turned slow, mysterious. "You're right, of course. If we told all our surprises, they really wouldn't be surprises."

Curiosity in his eyes, he tilted his head. "You gave in too easily. Have you got something up your sleeve?"

She blinked in wide-eyed innocence. "Me? Would I do that?"

Clearly enjoying this side of her, his smile returned. "Nah, I guess not."

Again her smile was cryptic. "Good. And I was afraid the elephant would be too much for you."

Incredulousness, disbelief, then dawning awareness crossed his face. "Kealey? Good one. You got me."

She started to turn away, then glanced back over her shoulder, lifting her brows in a nonchalant manner. "And I was worried that the *pony* was too messy..."

Kealey took one step forward. But Luke was

quicker. Before she could think, he'd picked her up, looping one arm beneath her knees, the other around her shoulders. Then they were twirling, round and round. Shock held her quiet for a moment.

His laughter, however, was too contagious to resist. And she found herself linking her hands behind his neck as they howled with laughter and spun some more.

When they were finally breathless, Luke stopped twirling. But he didn't put her down. Instead, their bright gazes connected. And she could almost feel the touch of his lips before they met hers. It was a slow kiss, one that sent her heart spinning.

The noise of happy children, relatives, clowns and ponies faded. Their world seemed suddenly small, undeniably distanced from anyone or anything. When their mouths eased apart, their gazes remained locked together.

Luke could see so much in her eyes. Something had cracked the impenetrable barrier she'd erected. He wondered if she was aware of the change. Or if she still believed she could keep her distance.

He wanted to wipe away the last of her fears, to convince her that he wouldn't be like the people she'd known in the past, that he could be trusted and counted upon. But all he could do was hold her in his arms, wishing he never had to let go.

Her lips began to turn up in a tremulous smile. He bent toward her again, but he felt a sudden tugging on the leg of his jeans.

"Me, too!" Hannah was saying. "Pick me up, too!"

Regret flowed between Luke and Kealey before he reluctantly set her back down. Unable to completely release her, his hand lingered on hers before he turned to young Hannah.

"Turn me in circles, too!" she cried.

Obliging, Luke spun the child as she giggled and shrieked happily.

Kealey watched, knowing the care he felt for these children was more genuine than anything she'd ever witnessed. No wonder she loved him. He was a rare man, one she suspected would love without reserve, one she wished she could have for all time.

But time wasn't on her side. The adoption process was moving forward. And when it was complete, she would no longer be needed. It would be time for her to move on to another life of loneliness.

Just then Luke released Hannah, sending her scampering toward the other kids.

"The pony ride was a great idea," Mary spoke from beside her.

Miles away, Kealey started at the unexpected comment. Yet she managed a reasonable smile. "I'm glad the kids like it."

"Like it? If it was put to a vote, they'd elect you Santa Claus."

The words warmed Kealey even further—until

she realized she was completely losing her grip on a lifetime of control.

But Mary didn't allow her to wallow in her thoughts. "You've made Brian one happy little boy."

"He's been through far too much for a child his age," Kealey responded, remembering the pain of forgotten, ignored birthdays.

"That's difficult, isn't it?" Mary asked, a deep instinctive wisdom shadowing her eyes.

Kealey averted her gaze. "Every case is different."

Mary took the hint gracefully. "I don't know how you and Rachel do it. I'm afraid I'd want to bring every unwanted child home with me."

"I do, too. But there isn't a house in the land big enough for all of them."

Mary nodded. "When I think of all the couples who are praying daily for a child, it seems hard to believe so many are thrown away by their parents."

Kealey couldn't reply. The pain of being a throwaway never lessened.

"I know, like these kids, there are accidents that take away the parents," Mary amended her words. "Still…"

Kealey finally found her voice. "Each unwanted child deserves a real home."

"Like the one you and Luke have provided for these three," Mary replied.

"Well, it was Luke—"

"He didn't stand a chance of getting them without you. And don't even try to tell me that it was something you usually do. As you just said, it would take a house larger than any in the land to hold them all."

"This was a special case," Kealey attempted to rationalize.

"Luke's lucky to have found you," Mary replied. "I know I'm the overprotective older sister, but I've always worried that he would end up with someone who would take advantage of the fact that he's so generous, always playing the role of rescuer." Unexpectedly, calm unflappable Mary was fighting tears. "I'm really glad you're part of our family." Then she hugged Kealey fiercely before moving away.

Speechless, Kealey could only stare after her. *Part of our family.* The words resounded long after Mary walked away. Did they really feel that way about her? Desperately, Kealey blinked away the tears in her own eyes.

Luke called out to her then. Surreptitiously swiping at her eyes, she took a deep breath and turned around. Seeing him wave her over to the long set of tables, she approached, inwardly telling herself to get a grip. But she had a terrible feeling that was getting damn near impossible.

"It's about time for cake and presents," Luke told her. "The man told me it's a good idea to let the pony have a little break. The kids can take some more rides after we eat.''

''Sounds good,'' Kealey replied in what she thought was a normal tone.

But Luke's instincts were too finely honed by now. ''Is something wrong?''

''No.'' She considered her words, then simply told the truth. ''I'm just surprised once again by how kind your family is.''

He reached an arm around her, drawing her close for an instant. ''They think you're pretty terrific, too.''

She attempted a watery smile, and Luke hugged her again, this time not saying anything, just offering her support.

In short time, the adults pitched in to round up all the kids and get them seated at the long tables. Brightly colored paper tablecloths were weighted down with equally colorful race-car-emblazoned paper plates and napkins, along with heavier containers filled with bouquets of mylar balloons on sticks, enough for all the kids.

It took two of Luke's brothers to carry in the gigantic cake. The sight of it evoked oohs and aahs from all the kids. Brian's eyes widened as though it were made of gold. Even Bentley barked in approval.

Ruth and Rachel began scooping up the ice cream and filling paper cups with grape punch. After the candles were lit, a rousing chorus of ''Happy Birthday'' was sung. Expectation and hope filled Brian's face before he drew in a huge breath and easily blew out all ten candles to a round of applause, hoots and whistles of approval.

Still beaming, he cut the first piece of cake. Kealey then took over the chore, with many ready hands helping to pass around the slices.

It was nice, Kealey realized, this unasked for supply of help. Glancing around she saw the genuine concern for her, the newest member of their family. Surely, some, if not most of them, had already made other plans for the day. Yet, without exception, they'd all turned out for the party.

Kealey shouldn't have been surprised, yet she was touched to see that everyone had brought presents for the ''half-year'' birthday boy. Brian squealed as he carefully unwrapped his first gift. But then, excitement catching, he ripped into the next one, part of a huge, seemingly endless mound.

As Kealey watched, her bottom lip tucked beneath her teeth, Jane came up and slipped an arm around her waist. ''This really was a lovely idea, dear.''

''Luke and I thought of it at the same time,'' Kealey demurred.

Jane chuckled, a laugh much like her son's. ''You're a treasure in today's world.''

Kealey blinked. ''I am?''

''Someone who's unwilling to take credit for wonderful ideas, plans and gestures, I'd say so.''

Kealey couldn't summon a reply.

But a moment later Luke strolled close by, taking a stance on her other side. "Do you mind if I steal my bride?"

Shaking her head, Jane smiled, then stepped away.

For a moment Kealey wondered if he had sensed her distress. As immediately she dismissed the notion. It was pure wishful thinking to imagine he was so in tune with her feelings.

"It's wonderful watching Brian, isn't it?" Luke murmured, in a quiet voice that couldn't be overheard.

She couldn't verbalize *how* wonderful she thought it was. Almost as if they'd provided Santa Claus, the Easter Bunny and the Tooth Fairy, but even better than that. So very much better.

Luke reached for her hand, holding it within the shelter of his. And for a moment she could almost believe her earlier wishful fancying.

"Even though that pile of presents looks endless, I'd better go get ours," Luke whispered.

Unlike the pony and clown, they'd discussed this part of the party. While Kealey continued to oversee the distribution of cake, Luke stole away to the garage.

Brian finally got down to the last of his presents. He was delighted by what Jane and Timothy had chosen—a microscope.

"Luke was always fascinated with science. And

since you love animals as well, maybe you'll find it fun, too," Timothy explained.

Clearly pleased by the comparison, Brian smiled as he carefully set the microscope on the table so it wouldn't get knocked over.

Then Luke pushed their gift forward. Brian's eyes widened to an impossible size.

"Mine?" he squeaked in awe.

Kealey and Luke both smiled.

Brian leaped up from the table, unable to reach his present fast enough.

A huge blue-and-silver bow sat atop a gleaming new bicycle. Ignoring the bow, Brian adroitly climbed on his new prize.

When he could finally speak, it was only a single syllable. "Wow!"

Finally dragging his gaze from the bicycle, Brian sought Luke and Kealey's gazes. "Thanks. I mean lots."

Luke stepped forward, his hand grasping Brian's shoulder. "You're welcome, son."

And he was Luke's son, Kealey knew suddenly, as she held back her emotions.

They were a family, one she was clinging to. And one she would give her life to keep. But could she still hope that Luke would want her to stay? Or was this the beginning of goodbye?

CHAPTER FIFTEEN

AUTUMN HAD FINALLY arrived in central Texas. It was the most perfect time of the year, in Luke's opinion. And, if he'd had poetry in his soul rather than science, he would have waxed on and on. Instead, he spent as much time as possible outside amid the changing colors. There he inhaled the best of smells, those of freshly fallen leaves on damp earth, along with the shifting aroma of the newly scented air, one that foretold of the coming winter, but promised more days of glorious sunshine.

Luke collected pumpkins of every possible size, along with squashes and gourds of the most exotic persuasions. Some resembled bumpy, little gnomes while others had glorious and earthy colors to recommend them. He wanted a big collection because, unlike most people, Luke didn't limit the carving of pumpkins to simply Halloween. For him it was a hobby for the entire season.

In most ways, this was a happy time. The kids were doing well in school and they'd found a place within his life, his family and the neighborhood.

Only one thing marred his favorite season. The waiting period before the final adoption was coming to an end. And even though he thought he was coming to know Kealey's heart, she'd yet to tell him how she felt. Their passion was as fresh and fervent as the first time, maybe even more so. Because lately he'd sensed a sort of desperation in her touch, as though she feared letting go.

She did still speak of the arrangements they would need to make after the adoption was final. And each time she spoke of their parting, his own heart splintered a little more.

Glancing across the yard, he watched as she played hide-and-seek with the kids among the trees and newly raked piles of leaves. The children, giggling loudly, dashed from spot to spot, loving every moment of the game.

When Troy hid beside one of the taller piles, Kealey tossed a few leaves over him, pretending not to see him. He giggled madly as she brushed away a few more leaves; then he jumped up in glee.

Drawn closer, Luke watched the glint of the afternoon sun on her golden hair. She'd allowed it to grow longer and it fell in gentle waves to the middle of her back. When she turned he could see that the fall colors made her remarkable eyes seem vibrantly green.

Breathless from running, she paused when she saw his gaze linger. "You can come play instead of doing all the work."

Responding to the open smile on her face, he approached. "You're right. Working should be avoided at all costs." His eyebrows rose a notch. "Especially when we can play."

"Tell you what," she offered, still catching her breath. "You play hide-and-seek and I'll rake leaves."

He screwed his expression into one of great concentration. "I don't think so."

A belated light in her eyes told him she'd just surmised his intent.

Before she could flee, he reached out, plucking her from the ground, then turned before dropping her gently into the largest pile of leaves.

"No, no!" she protested between wild bursts of laughter and gasps of injured indignation, flailing her arms uselessly.

He responded by stuffing her blouse with mounds of leaves.

"Stop, that tickles!" she managed to say between bouts of breath-snatching giggles. "And itches!"

"You don't say," he responded, goaded on by the response.

Fearlessly, she pitched handfuls of leaves at him, showering him soundly.

"Uh-oh. Now, you'll really have to pay."

Unable to stop laughing, she tried to scramble away, but his arms trapped her.

"Big man," she taunted.

"Bigger than you," he agreed mildly.

Belligerently she stuck her tongue out at him.

"Now that's a defense if I ever saw one," he responded.

She halfheartedly kicked her legs a bit more, her laughter fading as his gaze became intense. Her tongue retreated, but her mouth was poised in an open, questioning way.

Unable to resist, Luke lowered his lips to hers, tasting the now familiar essence of Kealey mixed with the warm flavor of autumn and sunshine. It was the best of everything. The perfect season, perfect day, perfect woman.

Her struggles ceasing, she allowed the kiss to go on and on. And Luke realized he could have kissed her until the sun moved past twilight, past dusk...past forever.

Returning gradually to reality, he lifted his head. Her eyes had transformed to emerald.

Searching her face, he absently plucked a few leaves from her hair. Flung wildly into the backdrop of the multicolored leaves, her hair was as alluring as if it were framed by silken sheets.

Just as unexpectedly, she reached up to trace his jaw, her touch as soft as the breath of summer. He wished the caress could go on forever. That, some-how, he could convince her to remain with them... with him.

"My turn!" Troy demanded.

Glancing up, Luke and Kealey saw the children's curious faces watching them.

"People kiss on TV sometimes," Hannah informed them.

Kealey's lips trembled in unexpected amusement.

"So they do," Luke replied. "And so do parents. Let's go attack those pumpkins."

"What about the leaves?" asked ever responsible Brian.

Luke looked around at the piles, then smiled. "They'll be here tomorrow. Come on."

The backyard table was covered with a collection of pumpkins and a few intriguing-looking gourds. Luke had purchased child-safe carving instruments for the kids.

"You sure we don't hafta wait for Halloween?" Hannah questioned. "It's nearly a month away."

"Positive," Luke replied.

"Should we save one?" Brian asked, not having completely shed his mantle of responsibility.

Kealey, so in tune with his feelings, gave him a small hug. "What if we carve these now and then at Halloween we get enough for us and also take some we've carved to the children's hospital?"

Brian didn't have to consider her suggestion for long. "Yeah. That'd be neat."

Yes it would, Luke acknowledged, again marveling at her generosity of spirit. Then he started helping the kids, showing them how to use the tools.

Each chose a different sort of design to carve. Luke studied his own pumpkin for a few moments, but he already had a design in mind.

Luke couldn't help noticing that Kealey stared at her pumpkin for an inordinately long time.

"Something wrong?" Luke asked.

She shook her head. "Not exactly. I haven't done this before. I watched you showing the kids, but I'm not sure what to carve myself."

Amazed, he could only stare at her. How had any American kid been able to reach adulthood without carving a pumpkin? Covering the sadness he felt over her stolen childhood, he passed her the book of designs he'd given to the children.

"I know they're usually faces. But do they have to be?" she asked.

"I don't see why."

"Okay." With deliberate precision she picked up her knife, her face screwed into lines of concentration.

Touched by this simple, but telling admission, he had to drag his attention back to his own task. He discarded his original design, instead thinking of a far better one.

The time passed harmoniously, the kids getting into the fun of pumpkin carving. With a few covert glances, Luke could see that Kealey was getting into it as well. More than an hour later, everyone was about done.

Luke, accustomed to carving dozens of pumpkins for his nieces and nephews, had become adept and quick at carving. It was how he'd come to view it as a seasonal pastime, rather than a one-day event.

He enjoyed the creativity, the uniqueness of each gourd.

"Mine's a fairy princess," Hannah announced. She'd made a good, if crude attempt, at a crown above the jagged eyes.

"So it is," Kealey exclaimed. "It's very pretty."

"But they're supposed to be scary," Troy protested, showing them a more traditional carving of a goblin.

"They can be anything you want them to be," Luke replied. "Scary, pretty, unique, realistic."

"Kealey, let's see yours!" Hannah demanded.

"I'm kind of new at this," Kealey explained as she pivoted the pumpkin to face the others.

They stared at it quietly for a moment.

"*H* like my name!" Hannah exclaimed.

"And *B*," Brian added.

Troy scrunched his face up, not as proficient in reading yet as his older brother and sister. "And a *T?*" he asked.

"Looks like it," Luke confirmed. Then he glanced at Kealey. "That's what I meant by unique."

Kealey looked as though she'd passed some sort of test. Again, Luke wished she could truly relax, but then he supposed that would be like asking him to ignore anyone, man or animal, in need. Her experience simply wouldn't allow it.

"Nice," he told her quietly as the kids examined each other's pumpkins.

She shrugged, but looked pleased. Then she turned suddenly to Brian. "We almost forgot to look at yours."

Reluctantly, Brian turned his around. Although it was crude, it was clear he had attempted to carve a dog.

"Why that looks just like Bentley!" Kealey exclaimed.

"It's not that good," Brian protested while at the same looking as though he wanted to be convinced her words were true.

"It's neat!" Troy told him loyally.

"Yeah," Hannah added. "Can you do one of Miss Tansy, too?"

Brian's smile vaulted into a grin. "I could try."

Kealey watched them for a moment, then carefully turned to Luke. "Hey, wait a minute. You're supposed to be the master. So where's your pumpkin?"

The kids also looked at him expectantly.

"You have to remember I sometimes use a different technique, just barely cutting into the skin of the pumpkin, rather than carving true holes," Luke explained.

"No stalling, mister," Kealey prodded him. "You made us all show ours."

Luke didn't mind revealing his carving. He just wasn't sure how Kealey would respond. Carefully he turned it around so they could all see.

And was greeted with dead silence.

Then Hannah grew excited, her voice high and light. "It's Kealey!"

"Yeah," the boys agreed a beat later, still studying the unusual design.

But it was Kealey's reaction he was waiting for.

She blinked, a growing sense of wonder suffusing her features. "Luke?" she questioned, in a quiet, faraway voice.

"I'm no artist, but, yeah, I tried to make it of you."

She bit down hard on her bottom lip, rapidly blinking her eyes.

As he'd said, Luke had lightly carved his portrait onto the outer shell, using the dark, outer skin as shadow and the inner skin as highlight. And in the light and shadow, he'd drawn a fair depiction of Kealey's face. Her long flowing hair was flung back and her eyes looked as though they were focused on something distant.

He'd also carved a good replica of her thin, perfect nose, her strong chin. But he'd given in to one impulse. She looked entirely delicate, a nearly whimsical fey creature.

"Wow," Brian finally said, breaking the silence.

"It looks pretty, just like you, Kealey," Hannah added.

Kealey, however, continued to stare at it until finally lifting her gaze to Luke. Then her voice was so quiet he had to lean closer to hear the brief words.

"Thank you."

Only two small words, but from them Luke took hope. Maybe, if he was very, very lucky, hope would be much of what he needed.

OCTOBER WAS SPEEDING by with undaunting swiftness. Throughout the previous months Luke and Kealey had passed the inspection visits by Children's Services with flying colors. In fact, the caseworker had remarked on more than one occasion that she'd rarely seen such a loving home, nor a couple so ideally suited.

When a second caseworker for the adoption process was assigned, he seemed surprised by the fact that Luke's name was the only one on the adoption papers. But it wasn't part of the process for him to question that oddity, only to assure that the home was satisfactory.

He understood that waiting to add Kealey's name to the adoption papers was probably a well-considered decision in light of the brevity of their marriage. Not that he felt that was a deterrent. In his estimation, they had provided an ideal home.

During that last adoption interview, Kealey had squirmed in her chair, desperately wishing she didn't have to be involved in the process. It was difficult enough to know the time was ticking away. Trying to keep ignorant of the stage the adoption was in was her only protection. Logically, she knew it wouldn't prolong her own time with Luke and the children she'd grown to love. These days, though, she was losing her grip on logic. It no longer seemed the proper barometer with which to gauge her life.

She'd also taken to using more and more of her annual leave, requesting a few hours each afternoon so she could be home to greet the children. After the adoption, she wouldn't need vacation time. She would work to fill the empty hours.

Today, however, she refused to think beyond the moment. She was using Luke's mother's recipe for oatmeal cookies. Their fragrant aroma wafted through the house and even Wayne had escaped from the clinic long enough to filch a few.

Halloween was only a week away and she planned to get a head start on learning how to make the best possible treats. She was nearly as excited as the kids about the upcoming holiday.

Hearing the back door open, she turned with a smile. But seeing Hannah's stricken, tear-streaked face, Kealey dropped the pan of cookies and rushed to her side. Brian held his sister's hand, though he looked up at Kealey helplessly.

Scooping up the little girl, Kealey smoothed the hair back from Hannah's face, then patted her back in comforting circles. "Shush," she told her gently as she made her way to the comfy chair in the corner of the kitchen. "It can't be that bad."

Hannah gulped and cried some more.

Kealey looked at Brian in question but he shrugged. "I dunno. Some kids were saying something to her and then she started crying and ran home. I caught up with her, but she just cried more.''

"You did the right thing, Brian, making sure she got home safely." Kealey rocked young Hannah back and forth, waiting until the child's sobs eased. "You can tell me what it is, sweetie."

For a while Hannah continued to cry. Then she lifted her head from Kealey's shoulders and gulped, her words barely legible between her sobs. "They said we didn't belong to anybody."

Kealey's reaction was fierce and quick. "Of course you do. You belong to us. To Luke…and me."

"Sure, Hannah," Brian added helpfully, his eyes lighting. "There's 'adopted' papers on Luke's desk."

Hannah was shaking her head. "But the kids said—''

"I'll show you the papers, okay?" Brian asked, trying to stop Hannah's tears.

"See," Kealey responded, managing to keep her own voice bright, despite the agony of Brian's words. "Now, doesn't that prove you belong to us?"

"I guess so." Hannah looked up at her, huge blue eyes swimming in tears. "Do you really want to keep us forever?"

More than this child would ever know, Kealey thought, biting down on her lip so hard she could taste blood. Using every scrap of willpower in her possession, she continued to make her voice light, convincing. "Of course. We love you."

Hannah stayed with Kealey in the chair, needing to be near someone she trusted. Kealey stroked her soft, blond hair.

Kealey wasn't certain how much time had passed when finally Hannah sighed soulfully and sat upright. "I wish you'd be part of my forever family."

Unable to speak, she again smoothed the child's hair, fervently hoping that Hannah would always remember how much she loved her.

Brian pushed open the kitchen door, his hands filled with papers. "See!" he exclaimed triumphantly. "It's papers with our names on it that say we're going to belong to Luke."

Kealey froze, then remembered to try to act naturally in front of the children. But closing her eyes, she knew her days here were nearly finished.

The evidence lay in front of her in unforgiving black and white. A rough draft of the final adoption decree, stamped with Luke's attorney's seal.

"Can we have a cookie?" Brian was asking.

Kealey motioned with her head. "Of course. They're for you. And Troy should be home from kindergarten soon."

"Can we watch TV?" Brian asked. "We won't get crumbs on the floor."

She met his serious young gaze and nodded. "That's just fine."

Leaving their backpacks on the table, they collected cookies and glasses of milk, carrying them into the living room. As soon as they were gone, Kealey swallowed, inching her way over to the forgotten papers.

She stared at the words until they grew blurry from the tears streaming down her face. She didn't even realize she was sobbing, the tearing in her heart was so great. Nor did she notice the swinging door to the kitchen push open, then close silently. All she knew was that again she had to say goodbye. Only this time, she wasn't sure she would ever recover.

BRIAN DID HIS CHORES, absently petting the animals as he filled food and water dishes, then swept out the kennels. Only today he didn't prod his younger brother and sister to either help him or hurry through their own duties. Because his mind was too full.

Full with the memory of Kealey's face as she sobbed in the kitchen, holding the papers he'd brought in to show Hannah, papers he had failed to return to Luke's desk.

And Brian wondered, if somehow, it was his fault that she was crying. Heart heavy, he was late in completing his chores, silent as he put away tools and bags of food.

Luke wandered back into the rear of the kennels, wiping his hands. "Hey, Brian. You're out here kind of late."

Brian looked up at the man who had become his hero, and his lower lip began to wobble.

Luke studied him for a moment, then approached quickly. "What is it, Brian?"

Afraid to meet Luke's eyes, he looked down at the new tennis shoes Kealey had bought for him. He remembered her warm hug, the joy in her eyes. And he felt a tear escape.

Luke knelt down. "You can tell me, son, whatever it is. Remember what I told you when you first came here. Nothing you can do will ever keep this from being your home."

Brian chewed his lower lip, then swiped at the tears that wouldn't stop. "I think I made Kealey cry."

Puzzled, Luke pulled back, studying the boy. "Why do you think that?"

"I didn't mean to," Brian pleaded.

"Of course you didn't," Luke agreed. "Just tell me what happened."

Brian recounted what had happened to Hannah, how they'd come home, then Kealey's help.

"I don't understand, Brian. None of your part in that should have made Kealey cry. Maybe she was crying because she felt bad for Hannah."

Slowly Brian shook his head. "It wasn't then. It was after." His words stumbled. "After I brought in the papers."

Even more confused, Luke patted the little boy's back, coaxing out the words. "What papers?"

Brian looked guilty, ashamed. "I took them from your desk."

"Well, I'd rather you'd tell me first if you want something from my office, but it's not a federal offense. Now, what papers did you take?"

"The ones with our names on them," Brian mumbled. "I saw them when I was emptying the trash. I thought it would make Hannah feel better to see that you want to keep us and that we do belong. When she saw them, she stopped crying, but then later..."

"Yes?" Luke prompted.

"I went back to the kitchen to get my backpack and Kealey was crying. Hard." Brian's eyes teared up again. "Like we did when our mom died."

Luke nodded, pulling Brian close for a quick hug, then wiping away his tears. "First, I'm sorry you had to see Kealey crying like that. But more important, you have to know that you didn't cause her to cry."

Brian looked up at him with an expression that said he wanted to believe Luke's words but wasn't certain he could. "How do you know?"

Luke's heart quickened, despite feeling bad for Brian's pain. "Because it's a grown-up thing. I'd like to be able to explain it, but I think you're a little too young to understand. But, if I promise that you didn't make Kealey cry, will you believe me?"

Luke knew Brian had placed all the trust he possessed in him. And the boy was probably just as certain that Luke wouldn't fail him now. "If you say so."

"I say so. Now. Why don't you head into the kitchen and help set the table."

"Aren't you coming?" Brian asked, still anxious.

"In a minute. I have to make a phone call. Now, can you do me a huge favor?"

Brian nodded fervently.

"Put a big smile on your face. I think Hannah and Kealey really need that right now. Girls aren't quite as tough as us guys."

Again Brian nodded.

As he left, Luke headed into his office. Hope gathered—a rush so powerful it nearly flattened him. He was about to take the biggest gamble of his life and he prayed that he'd read the signs correctly.

CHAPTER SIXTEEN

THE WEATHER WAS PERFECT. As though specifically ordered for the best Halloween ever, the temperature was mild, the breeze almost nonexistent. The kids could barely contain themselves as they collected backpacks and lunches.

Luke had booked his last appointment for just before eleven, making sure his afternoon was clear. And he'd already instructed all three children that their chores were taken care of for the day, because Wayne had volunteered to do them. Luke intended to make sure his assistant's paycheck contained a handsome bonus. Wayne would protest, but some things were worth more than gold.

Kealey had taken off the day and spent the morning making caramel apples, popcorn balls, marshmallow-crispie treats, and cookies. The kitchen was beginning to resemble Keebler Elf Land. And she'd bought enough candy to supply the entire county.

"The kids won't be home for a while, will they?" Luke asked, entering the kitchen.

Kealey, bent over the oven, checking another batch of cookies, nodded. "About four more hours."

Luke glanced around at the counters. "Kealey, there are only three of them. You've made enough treats to feed a brigade."

She frowned. "I wasn't sure what they'd like."

Luke's own anxiety eased a bit. "You know we're acting ridiculous? It's not *their* first Halloween."

"But it's ours with them," she murmured, meeting his gaze, doing her best to repress her longing.

"Those imps get under your skin, don't they?" Luke questioned idly, still studying her.

Her busy hands paused and she looked out the huge bay window, but no amount of looking or searching would give her the answers she sought, certainly not the ones she hoped for.

"You're about done here, aren't you?"

She glanced around. "I guess so, except for the cleanup."

"That can wait."

Puzzled, Kealey drew her eyebrows together. "For what?"

"I have something planned for us this afternoon." He glanced at his watch. "In fact, we're due there in about thirty minutes. Can you be ready?"

She angled her head. "Not to be repetitious, but for what?"

His smile was enigmatic, almost sly. "You'll see."

Kealey sighed. "I don't want to leave this mess—"

He placed two fingers gently over her lips. "Please?"

She opened her mouth to protest.

He leaned closer. "Please?"

What was it about this man that made every bit of her insides turn wobbly? Of its own accord, her head nodded in agreement.

His smile widened. "You won't regret it."

It wouldn't be regret she felt. Only an endless, unforgiving longing.

About twenty minutes later they were in his car, headed into town. She still didn't know where they were going, but to herself she acknowledged she would go anywhere with him.

When he turned into the lot of a small vintage clothing store, though, she was completely baffled. "We're going shopping?"

His smile remained mysterious. "How did you get to your age without knowing a surprise means not telling what it is?"

Remembrance of their previous discussion about surprises had her wanting to chuckle, but she tried to keep a straight face. "Point taken."

Once inside the store, Kealey realized it was a delight, from the tasteful display of vintage accessories to a breathtaking ballgown she guessed must be from the 1930s or 40s.

A young, spirited woman greeted them from behind the antique display case, her pretty face breaking into a grin. "Well, hello, Luke!" Then she turned to Kealey. "And you must be Mrs. Luke! I'm Britney!"

Swallowing the rush of emotions being identified as Luke's wife caused, she smiled. "Kealey, please."

"Great to meet you. Luke's told me all about you, of course."

"Of course?" Kealey echoed, turning to peer at Luke who'd managed to put on the most innocent expression she'd ever seen.

"Oh, Luke's like family. His brother and my brother played college football together. Our families shared the same section forever. Of course I was just a little kid then."

Of course. Kealey shook back a taste of envy.

"Which is why Britney helped arrange my surprise," Luke finally explained. "She failed to mention that her brother went on to the NFL and made a not so small fortune. And he helped her set up this business."

"This is your store?" Kealey asked, impressed regardless of where the backing was obtained. The store was lovely, full of charm, obviously set up and decorated by a very talented person.

Britney bobbed her head up and down, her grin beaming. "I've always loved old things—movies, clothes, furniture. I have a few antiques, but I didn't really want a store big enough for a lot of pieces. And the clothes and accessories are my first love."

"Do you specialize in any particular period?" Kealey asked, fascinated in spite of herself.

"Absolutely. Primarily the 30s and 40s. They epitomize glamour and sophistication to me. The 50s brings in fun, too. You wouldn't believe the poodle skirt I just found."

Luke cleared his throat. "And she's found a little something for us, too."

"Us?" Kealey asked in surprised confusion.

"Today's Halloween, right?" he asked.

"Yes," she answered cautiously.

"Our first with the kids?"

"Uh-huh," she responded with equal care.

"So I thought it would be a great idea for us to have costumes, too."

Kealey stared at him, completely stupefied.

Britney, however, wasn't at all hampered by caution. "Come on back to the dressing rooms. Wait'll you see what Luke came up with."

Completely undone, Kealey allowed Luke to tug her back to the dressing area.

"I got to thinking," he was telling her. "About who we could be. I considered the usual, Anthony and Cleopatra, Minnie and Mickey Mouse, that kind of stuff. But then, I thought our costumes ought to suit us."

Britney reached for a hanger, holding up a vintage lady's tennis outfit, circa 1952. In her other hand, she held up a man's ensemble, a light-colored suit with a dark shirt and a light tie, also circa 1952, and frankly resembling something a gangster would wear.

Now completely baffled, Kealey turned to Luke in silent query.

His smile was gentle. "Pat and Mike," he explained. "I thought I could be Spencer Tracy and you could be Kate Hepburn." He took her hand. "That is, if you'll let me call you Kate."

Amazed and touched, she could only nod.

Britney replaced the clothes on the rack, then reached for a pair of lady's tennis shoes and a racket. "Now finding these from the same time period was quite a feat, but my middle name's 'never say die.'"

Kealey blinked away the threat of tears, managing to smile. "That must make filling out forms quite a lot of trouble."

Britney grinned. "I knew you'd be cool. Anyone Luke married would have to be. So do you like the outfits?"

"They're perfect," Kealey managed to reply. *Absolutely perfect.*

"I had Luke's measurements so I know his suit will fit." She eyed Kealey critically. "And Luke was right. You're built just like Katherine Hepburn. Yours should fit, too."

Britney turned to wrap up the clothes and Kealey lowered her voice. "You told her I was built like Katherine Hepburn?"

This time his grin was strictly male. "Why do

you suppose I picked Pat and Mike costumes? That way I get to see those great legs of yours.''

An unaccustomed flush warmed her cheeks as she nudged him. ''As I recall, she played golf in that movie, too.''

''Where would the fun in that be?'' he asked in mock horror. ''A long skirt or trousers?''

Despite herself, she smiled. If she'd ever imagined being part of a Halloween celebration, she couldn't have thought of more perfect costumes if she'd worked on it for months. Yet he had, this man who rescued strays, protected the weak and nurtured everyone.

Turning away, she pretended to study the front of the store. But it didn't stop the tears she continued to fight, ones that reminded her that this was what she would miss most. And that goodbye was looming.

KEALEY FUSSED with Hannah's wings while Luke adjusted the tail on Troy's dinosaur costume.

''What are you guys supposed to be?'' Brian asked for the third time, studying Luke and Kealey's unconventional costumes.

''We told you, characters from the movie we watched one night, a long time ago.''

Kealey glanced up, the memory of the first real night of their marriage flowing between them.

Even though he'd had an inkling of his feelings

at that time, Luke could never have guessed how very precious she would become to him.

Kealey glanced back down, making sure Hannah's pink-and-silver fairy costume was perfect. Then she knelt beside Brian. She adjusted the eye patch of his pirate's outfit, making sure it didn't impair his vision, then retied the bright sash at his waist. He squirmed a tiny bit, but it was clear he relished her attention.

Since both Kealey and Luke wanted to go with the kids and watch them trick or treat, Wayne had volunteered to hand out candy. Porch duty, he called it. And since his apartment was on the top floor of his building, few kids made their way to it. Even so, he'd left out a bowl of candy that morning.

Before they left, Luke made certain all the kennels and gates were securely locked and that the house pets were inside.

"Don't worry," Wayne told him, as they locked the final gate. "No one will get past me."

Luke was certain any punks who dared try would be extremely sorry they had.

The kids dashed to the door of the first house, their high clear voices piping out the traditional greeting.

"They're having so much fun!" Kealey exclaimed happily, watching them with unconcealed joy.

Luke turned so that he was facing her. "And how about you?"

With a self-conscious motion, she smoothed the short skirt of her costume. "I've gotten a few looks from some of the other parents."

"Of course. The men in this town aren't blind, *Kate.*"

She batted at him playfully with the decades-old tennis racket. "You're entirely too prejudiced, *Spencer,* and the looks I was referring to are from the women."

"Right on both counts. I'm definitely prejudiced and of course the other women are jealous."

Exasperated, she spluttered. "That's not what I meant!"

His smile was again tender. "I know, *Kate.* I know."

She swallowed visibly, casting her eyes downward. Before he could comfort her, the kids pounded down the sidewalk, faces flushed with excitement. "We got chocolate bars!"

"Yea!" Kealey responded.

"We'll have lots to share," Brian added.

Kealey gave him a quick hug. "This is *your* bounty."

Then they were off, canvasing the neighborhood, all people whom Luke knew by name, people he could trust. The children's bags were filling with a multitude of candy. Passersby admired Luke and Kealey's costumes, some genuinely delighted when they learned the origin.

"I think I've spoken to more people tonight than

I have since I moved here,'' Kealey told him in wonder. ''Except for work and your family, of course.''

''They're a pretty friendly lot,'' Luke replied. ''And there's still enough small town left in us to know our neighbors and talk to strangers on the sidewalk when we pass.''

Kealey's gaze was on the children, who had just rung another doorbell. ''I think that's wonderful. I don't imagine there are too many places like Greenville left. Rural towns are struggling to stay alive, some disappearing altogether. You're lucky to have this place.''

''It's your place, too,'' he reminded her quietly.

Was it the moonlight or were her now dark eyes overly bright? ''So it is.''

They were quieter as they finished the rounds with the children. Small footsteps finally began to drag as the moon rose even higher in the sky.

They didn't protest too heartily when Luke suggested they head for home. As little Troy wound down even more, Luke lifted him on his shoulders for the final two blocks.

Wayne, still on porch duty, stood up to stretch mightily as they approached.

''How'd it go?'' Luke asked.

''Just fine. Lots of takers.'' Then Wayne directed his words to Kealey. ''I think you've got enough candy left for next Halloween.''

Next Halloween. Right now they didn't even

know if they had next month. Perhaps not even next week. That depended on the court date.

Still, Kealey's smile was brave, genuine. "It was awfully kind of you to hand out the candy tonight."

"Oh, I get a kick out of it, too. And I like knowing the animals are all safe."

"Is Bentley still inside?" Brian asked anxiously.

"You betcha. Just waiting for you," Wayne replied. He took one step down the stairs. "I'll say good-night now."

"Thanks, Wayne. Oh, and don't show up early tomorrow morning," Luke warned him.

Wayne nodded as he moved out into the darkness.

"He'll be here early," Kealey commented.

"No doubt about it," Luke replied, carrying Troy inside.

All three children were yawning.

"Time for bed," Kealey told them.

Each clenched a bag full of candy. "But we wanna see what we got."

Kealey met Luke's gaze. When he nodded she relented. "Okay, but as soon as you sort through the candy, it's off to bed."

They scooted into the living room, each pouring out their bags of loot. They examined and compared, trading a few pieces, setting others aside.

"Do most children behave like this on Halloween night?" Kealey asked in a wondering tone. "If they eat very much of that, they'll never get to sleep."

"I don't know. We used to stuff ourselves silly,

but I don't think it ever kept us up all night. What about you? Did you ever stay up all night on Halloween?"

She shook her head, an unconsciously sad motion. "I'm afraid not." Then she glanced down at her tennis outfit. "In fact this is my first Halloween costume, my first time going trick or treating."

"Didn't your mother ever take you?" he asked, still aching for all she'd missed.

"I was really young when she was...still around." Her gaze rested on the children, her love for them as evident as the pain she still carried with her.

Luke again felt the weight of the decision he'd made, one he'd yet to tell her. And he guessed it wouldn't be the children who would fail to sleep that night. Within a short time, he was going to risk their entire future.

If he was wrong, Kealey would walk away. In fact, it would push her away. And he suspected the wondering would stand between him and a decent night's sleep until the moment he found out what she would do.

CHAPTER SEVENTEEN

THE FOLLOWING DAYS passed more quickly than anticipated, one pushing into the next until the time was gone.

Still, Kealey wasn't ready. Staring at Luke in disbelief, she wondered why he wanted to inflict so much additional pain. "I don't understand why I have to go with you to the attorney's office."

"I wouldn't ask you if it wasn't necessary," he replied quietly, his face drawn.

She wanted to cry out in anguish. It was all slipping away, she realized, the depth of her pain a near physical thing.

Luke was eager to establish his rights with the children, to become their legal father. And when that happened, she would be redundant, a sad social worker who had sacrificed her heart in the foolish hope that Luke would come to love her, to ask her to stay. In that moment, she felt exactly as Hannah had. She desperately wanted to be part of this forever family.

But, unlike young Hannah, Luke didn't have a place for her in his life. After all, she forced herself to remember, she was the one who'd suggested their arrangement and insisted it be temporary, certain she could walk away once the children were safely and legally in Luke's care.

But she hadn't counted on falling in love with him.

Aware he was waiting for an answer, Kealey reluctantly lifted her chin. "Of course I'll go." She swallowed, wishing the past months hadn't caused her to feel like a weepy melodrama queen, ready to burst into tears at a moment's trouble. She hadn't expected such a reversal of her behavior. But then she'd never expected someone like Luke.

Upstairs, she opened the closet door slowly, selecting one of her conservative business suits, ignoring the brightly colored clothes she'd added to her wardrobe in the past few months.

Once dressed, she opened her jewelry box, her hand pausing suddenly. The elaborately carved, oriental box had been a present from Luke. Along with just about everything inside. She'd owned only a watch and a few pairs of earrings when they'd met. Now the box was filled with necklaces, bracelets and earrings—none she suspected were terribly valuable, but still pretty. Luke had continued to give her tokens she would have to remember him by.

It *was* different from her assortment of homes as a child, she now understood. Luke had made a genuine effort. She was the one who'd come up short. It wouldn't do to appear ungrateful. Briefly closing her eyes, she reached for the gold necklace he'd given her and fastened it around her neck. Then she chose a pair of earrings.

Gently rubbing the gold ring that still circled her finger, she considered removing it. But she couldn't make herself pull the ring from her finger. It could stay on her hand until she moved from the house. Belatedly, it occurred to her that if she didn't run away from Greenville and let Luke know how devastated she was, she might be able to visit the children occasionally, to let them know she still cared, would always care.

Determination alone completed her preparations. She took a final look in the mirror, silently bidding this Kealey goodbye. Once downstairs, she poked her head into the living room, and saw that Luke was standing by the front window, staring out into the street.

Feeling like a master thespian, she forced her voice into a normal tone. "I'm ready. I hope I didn't take too long."

He turned to her slowly, his face even more drawn. Perhaps it was difficult for him to say the words. He wasn't by nature an unkind person. It might bother him to have to tell her it was over, that it was time for her to leave.

Marshaling the last of her strength, she vowed he wouldn't have to. As soon as they returned from the attorney's office, she would matter-of-factly discuss the end of their arrangement. She'd been laying the groundwork since day one. Now, it was time to finish what she'd begun.

Stepping toward her, his face didn't lighten. If anything, he appeared even more drawn. "No, you didn't take too long."

Nor would she linger long, Kealey determined. From past experience she knew she could run quickly, disappear as though she'd never been. Then she could allow a discreet time to pass before she asked to visit the children.

Their ride to the attorney's office on Main Street was quiet. Kealey stole a glance at Luke's face, but he seemed lost in his own thoughts.

They parked not far from the small Italian restaurant where they'd first danced together. Kealey felt her lips beginning to tremble and bit down fiercely, welcoming the distracting pain.

Luke's attorney, Allen Sims, was both personable and intelligent. He was equally well prepared. His immaculate desk was dominated by a solitary folder.

The children's adoption folder, Kealey knew. Packed with reports from Social Services, and the adoption caseworkers. She'd seen ones like it dozens of times. But never had it been so personal.

Mr. Sims opened the folder. "Everything's in order. Glowing reports along with the necessary paperwork." He glanced up, his gaze resting on them both. "All that remains, other than the formal court appearance, are the signatures."

Numbly Kealey heard and processed his words.

In the same state, she watched as Luke accepted a pen and began signing his name. Signing their end.

She should be rejoicing. Three wonderful children were about to legally obtain the best father they could ever hope for. And she wouldn't have had it any other way.

Yes, she reminded herself, the children's welfare was foremost. Yet Kealey couldn't still the small voice that wondered why she'd never been allowed any happiness. She could never retrieve her stolen childhood, but ridiculously she'd hoped...

She lifted her gaze to see Luke studying her. Once he had her attention, he extended his hand, the one holding a pen.

Hurt and puzzled, she glanced back at him in question.

"I think you should read the papers, as well," Mr. Sims told her quietly. "Pay careful attention to the signature lines."

Still confused, she glanced down at the papers, neatly placed on the desk. There were two signature lines. One for Luke. One for her.

"But I don't understand," she responded, looking from Luke to the attorney.

"I asked him to add your name to the adoption papers," Luke replied.

"It was easy enough to do since you'd been involved in all the court and children's services inspections and interviews," Mr. Sims told her. "I consulted with them. They had no objection whatsoever.''

Luke reached out, taking her hand. ''The question is, do you?''

''Do I?'' she whispered, completely undone.

''Yes. Do you object? Are you ready to walk away or do you want to stay? To be my wife, a mother to the children?'' Hope filled his blue eyes, need darkened them.

Kealey didn't know the tears had begun until they were wetting her cheeks, blurring her eyes, salting her lips. In the distance, she heard Allen Sims push back his chair, the hollow echo of his steps as he walked across the wooden floor, then the sound of the door quietly closing behind him.

This time she couldn't stop either the tears or the trembling of her lips. ''Do you really mean it?'' she whispered, nearly afraid to say the words aloud.

Luke pushed back his own chair, drawing her up with him as he rose. ''Oh, Kealey, don't you know? Can't you see what you mean to me? To all of us?''

Emotion clogged her throat, singed her reserve. ''I feel as though I'm dreaming...hearing what I want to hear.''

His hands tightened around her arms. ''But I need to know, Kealey. I need to know how *you* feel. All you've talked about is leaving.''

She opened her mouth, but her past clenched around her like a tight, unforgiving fist. Inside she was still the unlovable little girl that nobody wanted. A throwaway child—perhaps a throwaway bride.

Luke pulled her closer, so close she could feel the brush of his breath on her cheek. "Because I love you, Kealey. But I need to know that you feel the same way about me. Our marriage has to be about more than just the children."

Her heart stuttered. Feeling her breath leave as his soul touched hers, she lifted her head, moving back so she could meet his eyes. Tears slid down her cheeks as she looked at him in wonder. "You love *me?*"

Tenderness, coupled with strength, filled his eyes. "With everything that's in me." Gently he stroked the hair that fell across her cheek, tucking it behind one ear. "I know you, Kealey Fitzpatrick Duncan. I know about all your scars, all you've missed, all you've wanted, all you've never thought you'd have." He swallowed, his voice hoarse, gritty. "And I love you even more for it. And, if you'll stay, I promise I'll do my best to make it up to you, to give you what you want."

Her hand lifted, her trembling fingers caressing his jaw ever so softly. When she finally spoke, her voice was raw, naked. "You've just given it to me, all I want, all I need—your heart."

She lifted her lips to his, her tears wetting their faces, cementing their commitment. Shadows lengthened around the office, silhouetting chairs, desks and file cabinets.

Allen Sims, both discreet and understanding, didn't interrupt. Only when they finally opened the door, did he proceed with the completion of the adoption papers.

And in the growing twilight, their bond was set. Fragile connections...a wounded spirit...and a man of honor. With a family to build and hold.

JUDGE ALLRED STUDIED the papers before him. Despite his narrow, forbidding features, it looked as though there was a touch more kindness in his eyes this time. Finally, he looked at them above the rim of his half glasses. "So, Mr. Duncan and Miss Fitzpatrick, I see you're back. Excuse me, that's Mrs. Duncan."

Kealey glanced at Luke, then at the judge, her expression tremulous. This court appearance wasn't a mere formality. The adoption wasn't final—yet.

The judge continued to study them. "Let me say, welcome back to family court."

"Thank you, Your Honor," Luke and Kealey chorused together rather unevenly.

The judge glanced at the papers again, this time removing his glasses to study the three Baker children. Finally his gaze rested again on Luke and Kealey.

"It looks as though congratulations are in order, Mr. and Mrs. Duncan. Despite tremendous, and might I add in my previous opinion, impossible odds, you have succeeded in my requirement of establishing a home that, according to Children's Service, is textbook perfect.''

Kealey felt her heart thundering against her chest as she expected the judge to add a *however*. One that said somehow they hadn't done enough, that the children weren't to be theirs.

"However..." Judge Allred began.

Kealey's hearing dimmed, a dizzy feeling taking hold of her.

"...in this case," the judge continued, "it seems you've gone beyond textbook. I'm happy to say that you have met and exceeded all the requirements as ordered by the state of Texas." His words continued, the legalese spelling out that Brian, Hannah and Troy now belonged to them.

Judge Allred paused for a moment, again studying the papers. "And in accordance with the petition filed by counsel, their names are to be changed as follows, Brian Baker Duncan, Hannah Baker Duncan and Troy Baker Duncan." It had been Luke's idea to retain Baker as part of their names, to pay homage to the parents who had borne and loved them.

The children each stood as their names were called, disbelief converting to wonder, then leaping to joy as the judge ended the proceedings by wishing them all good luck.

Allen Sims shook each of their hands and somehow they managed to stumble out of the hearing room, then the courthouse, finally standing in the radiant sunlight of the tranquil late-autumn afternoon.

"This always has been my favorite season," Luke told them, the shock of having everything go exactly as they'd hoped for just now settling in.

Brian looked at him, his face the only sober one in the group. "Is it for real, Luke? Forever?"

Luke knelt, embracing this child who had carved such a deep place in his heart. "Forever, Brian."

The boy's smile eclipsed the brilliance of the afternoon sun. Then suddenly all of the kids were jumping around them in a circle, shrieking with happiness.

Luke's gaze found Kealey's. "Forever," he promised.

The chink of security fell into place for the first time in her life. Her search for self, for family, for love. Now it was all hers. With the man she loved, with the children of her heart. Reaching for Luke's hand, she mouthed the solitary and glorious word. "Forever."

EPILOGUE

THE AGED, weathered gazebo remained the architectural centerpiece of Luke's yard. Sunlight eased over the ancient structure, then sidled over the equally old rosebushes, coaxing deep waves of fragrance from the red buds.

Not much about the yard, or the preparations, had changed from the previous year. Except that the ceremony, the renewal of their wedding vows, was being held on Kealey's birthday, a month earlier than their anniversary. It was the best way he could think of, Luke had explained, to celebrate her birthday. And from now on, he promised, her birthday was going to be unforgettable. To make up for all the forgotten ones.

Kealey touched the pearl teardrop earrings Luke had given her the year before then lowered her fingers to the string of pearls Jane had again loaned her. Almost everything was exactly the same. Almost.

Jane smoothed the veil, lifting it to trail over the back of the satin dress. ''It looks wonderful.''

''Really?'' Kealey questioned.

"Yes. And you look beautiful in it." Then Jane's eyes began to tear up. "Thank you."

"For what?"

"For being the only daughter of mine who wanted to wear my wedding gown."

Her daughter. Sometimes, it still didn't seem real. But each day, in every way Luke was proving that it was, and always would be.

Kealey was grateful not only for his love, but for his incredible family who had taken her in as their own. "Now stop that. You'll have me crying next."

Jane reached out to hug her, despite the words. "You're too beautiful for tears."

"Thank you, Jane."

"It's my honor that you're wearing the dress."

"Not just for that. But for Luke. For raising such an incredible son...for accepting me, astounding warts and all."

Jane smoothed the lace of the veil. "Not warts, my dear. Growing pains. Your heart was still learning how to grow and to accept. Now, before we both get all weepy, I think we'd better wipe the thundercloud off my 'incredible' son's face. I'm afraid he thinks I've kidnapped you. He'll be sending out the Mounties any minute now."

"Shouldn't that be the Texas Rangers?" Kealey replied, her tender smile finally eclipsing her tears.

Once again, paper lanterns fluttered in the gentle breeze; the giant magnolia tree towered over the arched trellis that bloomed with bougainvillea and sweet strands of honeysuckle. Wicker furniture, looking as though it had traveled through time, was scattered near the weathered fences.

Luke was once again flanked by his brother, Peter, along with Troy and Brian. This time, however, all his sisters, along with Hannah, were bridesmaids. Kealey had grown too close to them to choose.

Timothy extended his arm, and once again they took a walk up the bridal path. This time, however, there were no nerves, only joy. And when Timothy handed her to Luke, she felt as though she'd come home. Their eyes met, not disconnecting as he moved their clasped hands, holding them over her stomach. There wasn't even a tiny bulge yet. And they were the only ones who knew this joyous, new secret.

It was still many months away, but they would have a new brother or sister for Brian, Hannah and Troy. Kealey had struggled with the painful decision to give up her work to become a full-time mother, still feeling the need to reach out to and help as many children as she could.

But she and Luke had found an alternative. They were opening their home soon to foster children. Brian, Hannah and Troy were now confident in their relationship, knowing Luke and Kealey to be their parents in every way. Their own good natures, combined with Luke and Kealey's guidance, which had taught them to help others, made them secure. Secure enough that they welcomed the idea of helping other children. And Luke, as well as Kealey, had enough love to share with many children.

The minister repeated the words that had first bound them, that now reaffirmed their love. Kealey had barely heard them the first time. Now they were imprinted forever in her mind, along with the joy of this day, this man and the new life he'd given her.

The minister's words completed, Luke and Kealey turned to face their family and friends.

At that instant, instead of the triumphant wedding march, the organist broke into loud strains of "Happy Birthday." And all the guests burst into thunderous, exuberant choruses of the song.

Not knowing Luke had planned the song, Kealey stared at them in shock. Then, throwing her head back, she erupted into joyous, spontaneous laughter. Laughter that only a year earlier had been restrained, almost nonexistent.

But this was her family, she realized with mounting elation. Her new life, her new love, her fulfilled hope.

Balloons drifted into the air, emblazoned with the words Happy Birthday. And Luke's brothers parted to reveal the wedding cake—one whose top tier was decorated with a smiling couple holding a huge banner, also spelling out Happy Birthday.

Then everyone was laughing. Even the dogs were barking in accompaniment.

As the noise accelerated, Luke reached into his pocket, withdrawing a worn, but elegant golden locket. Flipping it open, he revealed pictures of the children on one side, he and Kealey on the other. He reached to fasten it around her neck. "Happy birthday, darling."

"But this must be a family heirloom," she protested.

"Smart *and* beautiful," he replied with a tender smile.

"But you shouldn't give me family heirlooms!"

"What do you think the tortoiseshell dresser set is?"

Her eyes widened.

"It was my great-grandmother's." He gently encircled her wedding band. "As was this. And, of course, the tiny emerald earrings and the bracelet with the solitary sapphire, to match the changing colors of your eyes. They were my portion of the jewelry from my grandmother. Their value is in sentiment, since they've been passed down for generations."

Astonishment knocked the wind out of her. "But you never told me," she sputtered. "And that was when you hadn't told me how you felt, when you thought I might leave!"

He cupped the back of her neck, bringing her within a breath's span. "You needed treasures to call your own, things no one could ever take away from you."

Her bottom lip trembled treacherously. "But—"

Luke stilled the question with his lips, finally pulling back long enough to look into her eyes. "And I already knew I'd found my treasure."

And Kealey knew she'd found hers. Her forever love, family, and children. They were a treasure beyond compare. Treasures an unloved child never dreamed she would have. Meeting Luke's tender gaze, she fell in love with him all over again. And knew, beyond the slightest doubt, that she would again and again. Forever.

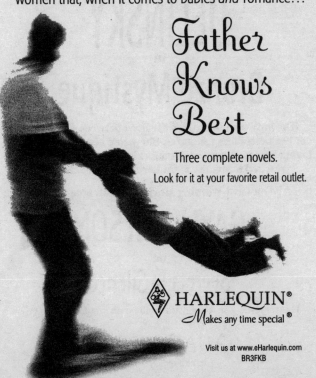

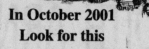

**In October 2001
Look for this**
New York Times **bestselling author**

BARBARA DELINSKY

in

Bronze Mystique

The only men in Sasha's life lived between the covers of her bestselling romances. She wrote about passionate, loving heroes, but no such man existed...til Doug Donohue rescued Sasha the night her motorcycle crashed.

AND award-winning Harlequin Intrigue author

GAYLE WILSON

in

Secrets in Silence

This fantastic 2-in-1 collection will be on sale October 2001.

HARLEQUIN®
Makes any time special ®

WITH HARLEQUIN AND SILHOUETTE

There's a romance to fit your every mood.

Passion

Harlequin Temptation

Harlequin Presents

Silhouette Desire

Pure Romance

Harlequin Romance

Silhouette Romance

Home & Family

Harlequin American Romance

Silhouette Special Edition

A Longer Story With More

Harlequin Superromance

Suspense & Adventure

Harlequin Intrigue

Silhouette Intimate Moments

Humor

Harlequin Duets

Historical

Harlequin Historicals

Special Releases

Other great romances to explore

This November 2001—
Silhouette Books cordially invites you
to the wedding of two of our favorite

YULETIDE BRIDES

A woman gets stuck faking happily-ever-after
with her soon-to-be ex-husband—or *is* she
faking?—all the while hiding their baby-to-be,
in **Marie Ferrarella's CHRISTMAS BRIDE.**

A man hired to bring back a mogul's lost
granddaughter goes from daring detective to
darling dad, when he falls for the girl *and*
her adoptive mother, in **Suzanne Carey's**
FATHER BY MARRIAGE.

Because there's nothing like
a Christmas wedding...

Silhouette®
Where love comes alive™

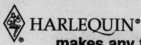

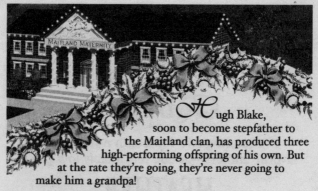

*H*ugh Blake, soon to become stepfather to the Maitland clan, has produced three high-performing offspring of his own. But at the rate they're going, they're never going to make him a grandpa!

There's *Suzanne*, a work-obsessed CEO whose Christmas spirit could use a little topping up....

And *Thomas*, a lawyer whose ability to hold on to the woman he loves is evaporating by the minute....

And *Diane*, a teacher so dedicated to her teenage students she hasn't noticed she's put her own life on hold.

But there's a Christmas wake-up call in store for the Blake siblings. Love *and* Christmas miracles are in store for all three!

Maitland Maternity Christmas

A collection from three of Harlequin's favorite authors

Muriel Jensen
Judy Christenberry
&Tina Leonard

Look for it in November 2001.